THE SPIRIT MACHINE AND OTHER NEW SHORT STORIES FROM CAMEROON

Edited with an Introduction by Emma Dawson

Critical, Cultural and Communications Press
ottingham
2009

The Spirit Machine and Other New Short Stories from Cameroon,
edited by Emma Dawson.

World Englishes Literature (Fiction)
General Editor: Emma Dawson

First published in Great Britain by Critical, Cultural and
Communications Press, Nottingham, 2009.

Cover design by Andrew Dawson.

ISBN 9781905510214

CONTENTS

MAP OF CAMEROON

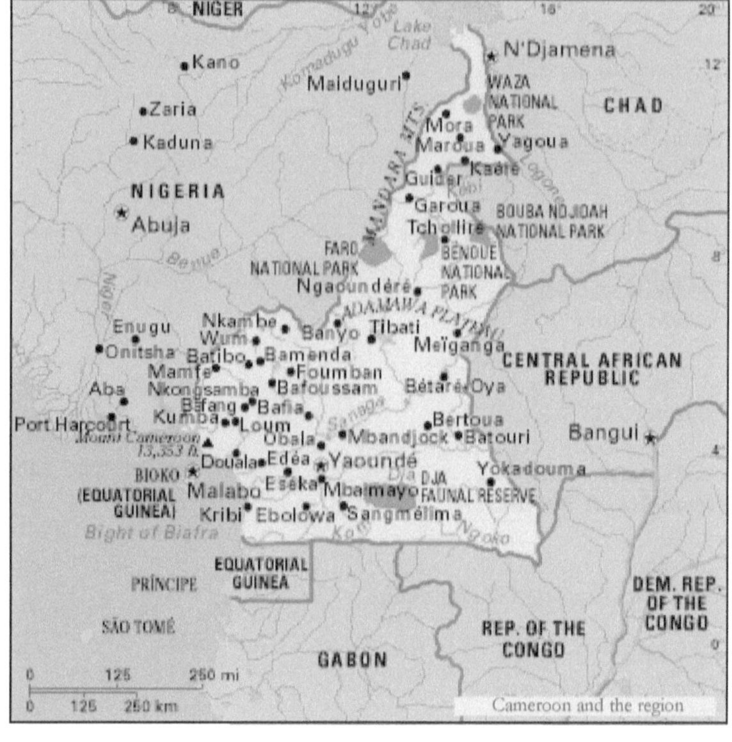

This volume belongs to the Fiction series of CCCP's World Englishes Literature imprint. This series focuses on the production of new writing in English, specifically new World Englishes fiction — a term which is defined in the introduction of each publication in the series. Country anthologies of new writing in English feature here, writing which is newly sourced, edited and presented with a critical introduction.

Each country anthology of new writing goes through a sequence of processes; firstly, a call for short stories is launched electronically through email lists of writers, writing groups, universities and other relevant organisations. Once submissions have been received and read, a journey to the respective country is arranged by the editor in order to meet with the writers who have submitted their work as well offer an opportunity for others who have not yet heard of the project to come along and learn about it.

Making the journey to the country in question is paramount and this is what makes the CCCP's country anthologies different from other anthologies of new writing in English. The journey to meet the writers is one that is made in order 'to listen' and not 'to tell'. The World Englishes Literature imprint as a whole explores being beyond the postcolonial, by 'listening' to those who know, who are writing the literature *now*. This stance diverges markedly from anthologies compiled using already published (and recognised) literature, as well as anthologies which are compiled from 'the Western armchair'.

The critical introduction to the country anthologies benefits from this act of 'listening' and, in doing so, aims to present an accurate portrait of the writing emerging from the country in question. The visit to the country also affords the editor an opportunity to research the history of the place and culture, emerging criticism and contemporary literary events, all of which concern themselves with writing in English. All discussions with writers, readers, teachers and other interested parties who contribute to the debate on writing in

English are audio-recorded in order for the material to be reproduced in a sensitive and accurate manner.

The final process is a re-opening of the call for submission within a limited timescale. This is conducted because very often, after the editor's visit to the country, writers continue to hear of the project and wish to submit their work. On the editor's return to the UK, the selection of entries is made in consultation with a second editor and reader. Selected writers are paid for their submissions.

The *World Englishes Literature Fiction* volumes are compilations of short stories which range from 3,000 to 10,000 words in length. The idea motivating such an anthology of short stories is to offer the reader an accessible and manageable 'taste' of a country's contemporary fiction writing in English. The short story also allows a country's writers to explore a variety of contemporary themes and concerns as well as exhibiting the linguistic diversity of the land in question.

Most of the writers presented in the country anthologies will not be 'known' to the Western reader and also possibly not even to many readers in their own countries This is a basic aim of the series: to promote new, emerging writers, often unknown to the West, writers who have not been 'endorsed' by Western publishing houses, but whose writing tells wonderful new stories in wonderful new ways.

Emma Dawson

ACKNOWLEDGMENTS

It started on a bright but chilly day in Corpus Christi College, Oxford, with Professor John Nkemngong Nkengasong in the SCR, a scrap of paper, a pencil and two languages – 'donc la rivière est là, entre les deux, so Cameroon is French and English then, je veux dire au niveau de la littérature'… Thank you, John; this anthology would not have happened without that meeting.

Ba'bila, thank you for your fascinating and riveting account of your writing life – I doubt that I will ever meet another like you! And of course for the CD mission – long live the voice of Bebe Manga! Eunice and Giftus, thank you for the warm welcome at the University of Yaoundé, the fine vegetarian fare. Eunice, thank you for that special Sunday, the songs still ring in my ears.

Tennu, the Malaria Doctor, thank you for your company and glasses of tonic!

Professor S.A. Ambanasom, I learnt so much from hearing your paper at the 5th ACWA conference, thank you. I remain your Austen-ised 'Emma'.

Thank you to all the writers who submitted in order to be considered for this anthology: keep writing, keep being who you are. A special thank you to the writers who feature here for working with me on editorial changes and considerations. I am honoured to have worked with you and to have produced *your* anthology.

Finally, M.D — in both name and position — when I first mentioned World Englishes Literature to you (quite some time ago now) you checked my use of the plural — thank you for continuing to check, revisit, redraft, and re-discuss this venture. I hope that you are as happy with the anthology as I am.

E.D.

For Cameroon –
I chose to listen…

INTRODUCTION

This introduction will begin by defining the term 'World Englishes' and explain how this relates to 'World Englishes Literature'. It will go on to address the situation in Cameroon, offering a brief history of writing in English in the country and the specific context of Anglophone writing, as it is often called. It will cite the major contributors to this movement. The introduction will conclude by outlining the nature of the contributions to this anthology, the writers and the themes that are present in this contemporary collection of new writing.

1. Defining 'World Englishes Literature'

The term 'World Englishes Literature' is inextricably linked to a field of linguistic interest, 'World Englishes'. The term 'World Englishes' is used to encompass the notions of 'new Englishes' and 'New Englishes' (Jenkins 2006: 22-23). According to Jenkins (2000: 22) 'new Englishes' resulted from the first diaspora, and are to be found in the United States, Canada, Australia, New Zealand and South Africa. By contrast, 'New Englishes' (note the upper case 'New') resulted from the second diaspora, and is understood as being the product of situations in which English has been learnt as a second language or is spoken as a language within a wider multilingual selection of languages: such scenarios would include, for example, Indian Englishes, Nigerian Englishes, Singaporean or Philippine Englishes. In short, not only is the linguistic production different of 'an English' and 'English as a Lingua Franca' (ELF), but the cultural, functional and ideological aspects are also at variance between the two.[1]

---

[1] See Tan *et al.* for further discussion on the difference between EFL and the Englishes of the 'Expanding circle' (specifically 2006: 84-94), as well as Kachru and Nelson for discussion on EFL versus ESL in an Asian context (2006: 25).

Introduction

Jenkins' definition of 'New Englishes' and 'the second diaspora' (2006: 22-23) may have been influenced by the earlier work of Platt *et al.* (1984) who referred to the phenomenon as a 'New English' (note the singular). According to Platt *et al.* the four defining criteria for a 'New English' are as follows:

1. It has developed through an education system. This means that it has been taught as a subject and, in many cases, also used as a medium of instruction in regions where languages other than English were the main languages.
2. It has developed in an area where a native variety of English was *not* the language spoken by most of the population.
3. It is used for a range of functions *among* those who speak or write it in the region where it is used.
4. It has become 'localised' or 'nativised' by adopting some language features of its own, such as sounds, intonation patterns, sentence structures, words and expressions.

(Platt et al. 1984: 2-3; original emphasis)

Thus Jenkins' notion of 'new Englishes' and 'New Englishes' (which supersedes the work of Platt and colleagues) are included in the understanding of 'World Englishes' for the purposes of this introduction and the imprint of which it is part.

Kachru's (1982) model helps to highlight the extent of the meaning of 'World Englishes', as his model of the Englishes of the world demonstrates that the 'Inner circle' (although it does include the UK) constitutes the 'new Englishes' (that is, the result of the first diaspora, according to Jenkins) while the 'Outer circle' constitutes the 'New Englishes' (that of the second diaspora). Kachru's model also offers a third dimension to the global production of Englishes, namely that of the 'Expanding circle'. In summary, Kachru's model (of Inner, Outer and Expanding circles) can be taken as wholly representational of what is meant here as 'World Englishes' language production.

Kachru's (1982) model of the spread of English around the world remains one of several base models from which we understand the tripartite *linguistic* phenomenon that is 'World Englishes': the Inner, Outer and Expanding circles roughly correspond to the concepts of English as a native language (ENL), English as a second language (ESL) and English as a foreign language (EFL) respectively. The

Inner circle includes the United States of America (USA), the United Kingdom (UK), Canada, Australia and New Zealand; the Outer circle includes nations such as India, Kenya, Malaysia and Singapore; and the Expanding circle includes nations such as China, Egypt, Israel and Japan (see Melchers and Shaw 2003, which devotes a detailed chapter to each of the three varieties).

Even in the Inner circle — that is, countries in which English is the native language — other languages may be spoken. In order to demonstrate how these languages are different from the dominant language, I will identify them as 'diaspora community languages' (see Karla *et al.* 2005 for diverse discussion on notions of 'diaspora and hybridity'). In the United States, Spanish, Italian and Hebrew are spoken (and written) as diaspora community languages. In the United Kingdom, languages such as Hindi, Punjabi, Gujarati, Bengali, Urdu and Jamaican patois are spoken (and often also written). Numerous other languages of diaspora communities settled from first generation to third or fourth generation in Canada, Australia and New Zealand can also be similarly categorised. Moreover, any amalgamation of either a 'diaspora community language' or a language *per se* with the 'English' of an ENL country will therefore produce yet another 'English'. For example, in the UK, British Asian English is categorized by its own lexemes, phonology and grammar, but British Asian English shifts and changes, depending on whether the variety of British Asian English is spoken by people of Pakistani origin or, say, of Indian origin. Equally it differs (in regional accent, grammar and/or lexemes) depending on where in the country the variety is spoken.

In addition, within the Inner circle there are languages which do not bear description as one of Kachru's Inner circle Englishes or as one of the 'diaspora community languages'. These can be defined as 'native' although the term is semantically problematic. In the USA these 'native' languages are (American) Indian languages, while in the UK they are Scots, Welsh or Gaelic, and in the case of Australia and New Zealand these are languages of Aboriginal origins. There are many indigenous or 'native' languages of these lands that I have not mentioned here, but I trust that this brief overview of the language situation(s) in the Inner circle has illustrated sufficiently the complexities of Kachru's notion.

In summary, we can see that Kachru's model is helpful in conceiving of the Englishes of the world and accommodates, to an extent, the complex situation of the multi-Englishes of the Inner circle. Can, therefore, this notion simply be transferred to the formation of 'literary' uses of World Englishes? My own answer to this question perhaps curiously, is no. Indeed, I would wish to dismiss the 'Inner circle' notion, which is undeniably applicable to language use, as unhelpful in explicating World Englishes *literature*. When the *linguistic* voices (of World Englishes speakers) become *literary* voices (of World Englishes writers), it is my own view that, while Kachru's 'Outer' and 'Expanding' circles remain useful concepts for an explanation of what World Englishes literature is, this is not so of the 'Inner' circle: in my definition, that is, World Englishes literature is *never* produced from the Inner circle.

The issues at stake in this argument are not simple questions of geography, spatial proximity to the English 'Standard', or characteristic linguistic properties: it is more how these matters, in a certain combination, produce varied kinds of writing, some of which I would call World Englishes literature, and some of which I would not (although they are all in play). The lines of this debate have long been drawn up in historic theoretical arguments around colonialism and postcolonialism and the conceptual role played in these debates by the voice of the 'subaltern' (Spivak 1988).[2] Likewise, there is often an assumption that writing from the Outer or Expanding circles is always to be explained by the nature of the 'gravitational pull' of the language of the Inner circle. But in my view the multiple features which determine the voice of a World Englishes writer are not defined by the notion of the voice being that of the 'subaltern' — whether geographic, linguistic, cultural, ideological, or all of the foregoing. World Englishes writers are less and less interested in their putative subalternity to a former colonial power and more and more interested in what constitutes, positively, the identity of the culture from within which they write. Similarly, they are less and less likely to worry as to the relation of the English they use to the

---

[2] .'Postcolonialism' or 'postcolonial studies' is understood to span many disciplines (history, cultural studies, ethnography), but for our purposes the term refers to its deployment within literary studies. The term will also be used without the (often deployed) hyphen. Boehmer (2005: 3) distinguishes between 'postcolonial' as being pre-Second World War and 'post-colonial' as being post-war. I shall not deal with 'post(-)colonial' notions of literature to the extent that differentiations of such nicety will be required.

notionally 'original' English of the Inner circle. I might therefore best encapsulate my definition as follows: *most (but not all) World Englishes literature explores the culture(s) of the country and people from which it is written (these countries belong to Kachru's Outer and Expanding circles); usually the literature employs the English of that place (to a lesser or greater degree); and, moreover, the writer chooses to write in that English over other languages in which she could alternatively write.*

It follows that World Englishes literature is not a synonym for postcolonial literature, although many countries with a history of (for example) British colonialism produce World Englishes literature. The voice of World Englishes literature is not one that necessarily laments postcoloniality or one that wishes for the 'subaltern to speak' (Spivak: 1988). Rather, World Englishes is (as it were) post-postcolonial, and although its writers may remember and even celebrate a defining moment of political independence from a colonising power (as in India in 1947, Nigeria in 1960, Kenya in 1963, or the Philippines in 1946), it also includes a generation of writers who do not.

In short, this anthology, and the imprint of which it is a part, invites readers to move beyond the appreciation of Anglophone writers in relation to their colonial past (which is, predominantly, the inflection which has been given to discussion of their work). It does so in the belief that there are many other avenues for discussion and appreciation of this enormous body of writing. I shall suggest some of these alternatives in the further discussion which follows.

2. World Englishes Literature In Cameroon

World Englishes writing in Cameroon, or 'Anglophone writing' as it is sometimes referred to, occupies a challenging, difficult and often dangerous place in a dominant Francophone nation. Cameroon, sometimes described as being located in West Africa, at other times as being located in Central Africa, has a bilingual, bicultural colonial history. From 1955 the struggle for independence was growing and, in 1960, Cameroon was declared an independent nation. The border between Eastern Nigeria and Western Cameroon has history – as part of Nigeria, Britain administered what was known as 'British Northern and Southern Cameroons' from 1918-1960. Britain 'inherited' the Western part of Cameroon and France inherited the

Eastern part after Germany lost it in 1914; the latter had previously been known as 'German Kamerun'. It is not surprising, therefore, that even today in Cameroon the Western part of the country is predominantly Anglophone (particularly the North West) whilst the central and Eastern parts of Cameroon remain predominantly Francophone.

The period from the late 1950s through to independence in 1960 marks the birth of 'Anglophone writing' in Cameroon. Sankie Maimo's play *I am Vindicated* (1958), a work which was actually published in Nigeria by Ibadan University Press, is indicative of this birth. Since 1958 a small number of Anglophone Cameroonian writers have been published by Nigerian presses, and even today the matter of 'publishing' Anglophone writing within Cameroon remains a contentious topic. Anglophone publishing houses *per se* are few and far between; a fact which impacts heavily on the dissemination of creative Anglophone Cameroonian writing. Yet production and dissemination must not be seen as one of the same; *production* of Anglophone creative writing in Cameroon is constant, indeed prolific. Witness Fonlon (De la Taille *et al.* 1986): 'There is an abundance of writing. What is lacking are the readers to buy the books, and the publishers to publish them' (160). Due to the fact that the *dissemination* of such works, importantly 'at home', but also abroad, remains restricted, a lot of Anglophone writing in Cameroon goes unknown and unread. Francophone publishing houses abound. These institutions are not always ready to publish works which celebrate what it is to be Anglophone in Cameroon nor, more evidently, works which challenge the cultural and social Francophone identity in Cameroon today. It does not come as a surprise, therefore, to read that the evolution of Anglophone writing in Cameroon has not always been an easy or a peaceful one.

Professor Bernard Fonlon, in the early 1970s at the Federal University of Yaoundé, encouraged many writers through his creative writing classes and literary competitions in short fiction. He is well known for his involvement in the *Cameroon Cultural Review*. Fonlon gives advice to those wishing to write in Cameroon: 'Be attentive to what happens in society and within yourself, so that what you produce is sincere' (1986: 160). Most importantly, though, Fonlon recognised early on the importance of 'the voice' of writing in English from African nations:

This new literature draws inspiration largely from African life and, thanks to its intimate knowledge of both modern and traditional Africa, it paints very authentic pictures of African life. The striking thing about the literature is that, not only is the content African but the foreign language through which it finds expression, is reshaped by the minds of the characters presented therein, and receives thereby a new imprint. (De la Taille *et al.* 1986: 176)

Professor Bole Butake, as a student at the University of Yaoundé, also edited journals in creative writing, encouraging a body of Anglophone writing to grow. Later in his career, in 1976, Butake started the journal *The Mould* because of the complaints at that time that Anglophones were not writing: 'I originally agreed with the idea that Anglophones were not interested in writing, so I founded a small group in a workshop situation. Maimo, Jumbam, and Abety used to attend out meetings. I later came to realise that Anglophones were indeed writing but the problem was to get manuscripts published' (De la Taille *et al.* 1986: 52).

Butake went on to co-edit the proceedings of the Workshop on Anglophone Writing in Cameroon, held at the Goethe Institute in Yaoundé in 1993. This workshop was a seminal event in the recognition of discourse on Anglophone writing in Cameroon and was the flagship for further workshops and conferences. The University of Buea hosted a conference on Cameroon literature in 1994; in 1999 the 3L Conference (Language, Literature and Liberty) took place at the University of Yaoundé I; and finally the birth of ACWA (the Anglophone Cameroon Writers' Association) had its first annual conference in Bamenda in 2003 and its second in 2004 in Buea. ACWA's fifth Annual Conference took place at the British Council in Yaoundé in 2008, as the association had missed its planned 2007 Conference, which was postponed due to unrest in the country.

The poet Professor Charles Alobwed'Epie's paper at the Goethe Institute conference in 1993 explored what is meant by the term 'Anglophone' and looked at the geographical and cultural aspects of being Anglophone in a predominantly Francophone nation: 'We cannot talk of Cameroon English if we are not proud of tailoring the English language to express those intricate realities of our home languages and that the Queen's language in its purity cannot express. This tailoring can only be done in our literature' (Lyonga 1993: 58).

Introduction

Professor Shadrach A. Ambanasom has also published widely on all aspects of Anglophone writing in Cameroon (on the novel, 2007, and on playwrights, 2003). At the fifth ACWA conference (2008), Ambanasom called for Anglophone Cameroonian writers to think about the challenges ahead. For the future of Anglophone literature in Cameroon, Ambanasom insists,

> We should first master our medium of expression, the English language. Though it can never be pure in our hands, given our post-coloniality, we should diligently assimilate its grammar and internalize the rules that govern its function so that when, in the exercise of our poetic license, we violate these rules, let this grammatical transgression be committed from a position of linguistic competence and not from syntactic ignorance and naiveté. I believe that, as creators and critics using English as a working tool, this is one of our major challenges: the mastery of our medium of imaginative expression. (2008, unpublished)

Ambanasom also calls for publishers to produce bigger print runs, as very often a book is sold out just as soon as it is published, and he also demands more engagement with criticism:

> Therefore, fellow creators and critics, cast aside your garment of fear, and put on your armour of objectivity and discuss the content of our literature objectively and fearlessly. For, beyond the critical character of their significant work, our most sensitive imaginative minds mean well for our country. Beyond their figurative discourse, beyond the metaphors, allegories and symbols in which their work is couched, the fundamental aim of their creative endeavour is this one moral imperative: to transcend entertainment and get to the level of instruction, to construct a better, fairer and more prosperous Cameroonian society.
>
> These committed dramatists and their counterparts in poetry, the novel, the essay, and the short story are real sons and daughters of Cameroon who have given the word 'patriotism' a new meaning. They rightly deserve our accolades instead of the cold, indifferent shrug of our shoulders. (2008, unpublished)

Professor John Nkemngong Nkengasong, current president of ACWA, is often referred to as a 'radical visionary' of Anglophone

Cameroon, as is demonstrated by his novels, short stories but most notably his plays. Nkengasong's work follows in the footsteps of the great dramatists Bate Besong and Bole Butake and the Theatre of the Absurd. His plays deal with complex social and political issues in Cameroon and the wider issue of 'Africa'. Facing head-on some of the social evils of society, such as corruption and dictatorship, Nkengasong's drama challenges the average Cameroonian's conception of the society in which s/he lives. The playwright Victor Epie Ngome also asks serious questions of the audience through his work. Although Epie's style is unlike that of Nkengasong and Besong, he still challenges the cultural and social inequalities of Cameroon. In his play *What God As Put Asunder*, he uses the marriage of two people to represent the political union of the Anglophone region and the Francophone region – a union wrought with diametrically opposed differences.

One of the most infamous plays of Anglophone Cameroon, *Beasts of No Nation*, written by Besong, and directed by Butake, saw Besong arrested in 1991, and yet a year later he was awarded the ANA award for Literature for his play, *Requiem For The Last Kaiser*. At the 1993 Goethe Institute conference, Besong exhorted:

> The Anglophone Cameroonian writer must never forget his origins. His writing must depict the conditions of his people, expressing their spontaneous feelings of betrayal, protest and anger. It must challenge. It must indict head on. His writing must open up the Chinese Wall of Opportunity, closed to his people for over three decades. Our literature must convey with remarkable force the moods of the Anglophone Cameroonian caught in the assimilation-nightmare of Sisyphean existence. (Lyonga 1993: 18)[3]

---

[3] Besong died on 8 March 2007. He was travelling from Buea in the North West Anglophone province to Yaoundé overnight in order to obtain a visa from the American Embassy, where he had an 8am appointment. Besong died alongside a well-known television producer and also a critic. The accident killed all passengers and the driver. During my time in Yaoundé talking to writers and critics, I found the time to ask Ba'bila Mutia, a well-known writer in Cameroon and friend of Bate Besong from university days, how he thought Besong would like to be remembered. Mutia shared the following: 'I think Bate Besong would like to be remembered as a champion or a pioneer of change. His plays were very provocative, his plays reflected the nature of the Anglophones, he was anti-oppression.'

As we have read here, Fonlon's enthusiasm and encouragement for creative writing in English in Cameroon helped to produce and recognise some excellent short story writers such as Bole Butake and Nol Alembong. However, successful writers with little or no direct contact with Fonlon have emerged over the years too: Eunice Ngongkum, Chop Samuel, and Ba'bila Mutia are just some of the names, two of whom feature here in this anthology. According to Tala Kashim (De la Taille *et al.* 1986: 187) it would seem that it is Anglophones who are ahead of the Francophones in this area: 'The short story appears to be one of the very few literary forms in which English-speaking Cameroonians seem to have an edge over their French-speaking counterparts.' Kashim's justifications for this claim include the recognition of Fonlon's work in the 1970s at the University of Yaoundé, encouraging young writers to experiment with the short story form, holding short story competitions, and publishing the winners. Kashim has also been influential in fostering writing talent among Anglophone Cameroonians. He is the founder of the journal *New Horizons*. In 1986, when asked about the aim of the journal, he answered: 'The journal offers me the opportunity and challenge to dig deeper into Cameroon literature and to try to be as knowledgeable as possible in my own field. It has both a creative and critical format to appeal to both students and scholars. We always aim for some articles of interest to the students' (De la Taille *et al.* 1986: 176).

Until recently the Cameroonian short story in English has often interested itself directly with postcolonial Cameroonian society. But things are changing, and as this anthology will hopefully demonstrate, many of the themes explored in the short stories are not directly linked to a sense of postcoloniality, but reach beyond that experience and into the lives of ordinary Cameroonians today. The stories do reveal the past that Cameroon has known, whether it is through the code-switching or the variety of language used or the themes that, when unravelled, lead back in some way to a legacy of colonisation. But as Fonlon has always insisted, the benefits of 'cultural borrowing' are great. Indeed, of Cameroon, with its bicultural colonial past, he writes: 'No people is self-sufficient; and, thus there is no inherent shame whatsoever attached to borrowing or exchange between nations. On the contrary, it is one of the most effective ways of promoting mutual assistance, mutual understanding, and mutual respect among peoples of the world' (De la Taille *et al.* 1986: 164).[4]

3. Write There, Write Now

This collection of short stories explores universal as well as local issues – the political, the personal, the scary, the serious and the profound all feature here. In the title story, Ba'bila Mutia takes us to a village where Gabuma, a young boy, is under pressure to perform *the gaze*. The arrival of the earth-moving machine will delay and yet (unknowingly to Gabuma) will also finally bring the boy to his fate – *the gaze*. The earth-moving machine upsets the tranquillity of the village and the villagers are undecided about its presence, for it promises development, but at what price? Gabuma becomes friends with the amulet-wearing driver of the earth-moving machine and spends time with him whilst he works in the village, but the friendship can't last for long and Gabuma's dreams are unsettling.

'The Lost Art' by Job Fongho Tende transports the reader to 2150 AD Yaoundé, Cameroon. Things have changed: religion is out and the State is in. The story follows the life of Meko, a sculptor, and his struggle between church and State. Through sculpture, Meko enters a universe where he finds his late father and many of the legendary forest people who came before him, because Meko's work opens vistas for the spirits to enter the world of the living. But there is one special sculpture, hiding away in Meko's workshop, his masterpiece – a masterpiece which brings him to irreversible consequences.

Mbuh Mbuh Tennu's 'The Betrayal' is also a story which explores the theme of religion, as a backdrop to the wider concerns of working in a bilingual environment at a university. Dr Alex Languid, depressed following the tragic death of his wife, is happily distracted by his 33-year-old secretary Mimmie, whose life is the machine she

---

[4] Cameroon and some of its World Englishes writers have featured in editions of *Palapala* magazine (**www.palapalamagazine.com**), notably in issues 2 and 4. The blog at **www.anglocamlit.blogspot.com** does not focus only on Anglophone writers within Cameroon but rather the diaspora too. However, it describes World Englishes Cameroon writers as 'writers on the homefront'.

types on and the Christian faith she holds so dear. But is Mimmie enough? What will Dr Alex do as he faces life changing decisions?

Eunice Ngongkum's 'A Lie Has A Short Life' is also set in a university context, the university of Vembe. Baamoh, six months from completing his BA in History, decides to ensure a bright future for all Univembians, even if this means sacrificing his own studies — after all, planning strikes and demonstrations takes time and commitment. Despite the warnings of gendarme-filled streets, Baamoh rallies the students in protest, but has it all been in vain?

'Sour Juice' by Sammy Oke Akombi is a story of money. Jacobo's orange trees look promising, and finally he has a sense of satisfaction from growing and tending all these months, because harvest has arrived. Ten bags of fruit, sixty oranges in each one – what a harvest! But when it comes to tasting the fruit all is not what it seemed. The orange juice is sour. Completely inedible, the harvest of oranges is of no use at all. He was so careful to plant, water and tend his crops, so why have his fields yielded sour fruit?

John Nkemngong Nkengason's 'Kakamba' introduces us to the eponymous hero, who, feeling unwell, visits the doctor. The Doctor enquires after Mr Kakamba's health and profession and then asks him directly if he is married. Uncomfortable with the Doctor's forthrightness, he answers, 'No'. She asks whether he has ever had an HIV test. Packed off to the lab with a Malaria form and an HIV form, he is instructed to have blood taken and to wait for the results.

Oscar Chenyi Labang's story takes the reader to a village where the inhabitants await the signal to embark on 'The Visit'. But Pa Ngeh has some advice, to which young men of the village sit down to listen. One of the listeners to the tale he subsequently narrates is Kungwe. Is Kungwe ready to be married, to become a 'responsible' man? Is he, after all, ready for the impending 'Visit'?

A detailed account of life as a civil servant is found in Florence Ndiyah's 'My First Million'. The files piled high on the desk, the uncomfortable office chair and the hot, sticky atmosphere in which he must work leave the civil servant Mr Sama Max at his wits' end. If only he could get a break, if only someone would give him that chance… Then, announced on the radio are the promotions made by the Head of State: Mr Sama Max is finally made a Minister and life's problems are solved. As time rolls by, however, he faces challenges that he had not anticipated.

Wirndzerem G. Barfee also deals with the life of a civil servant in

'Jury of the Corrupt'. The civil servant's name is Dongo. The constant code-switching between French and English in this story brings to life the reality of working as a *fonctionnaire* in a bilingual environment. Dongo's once-classmate, Manga, offers a solution to pull Dongo out of his miserable, penny-pinching *fonctionnaire* lifestyle. As it hangs in the balance, Dongo is unsure of whether to take it, what the consequences of accepting such a solution will be, and where will he find the million that will start the ball rolling?

What this brief overview of contemporary Anglophone literature in Cameroon offers is the opportunity to see that we are at a crucial juncture in its evolution. The new writing presented here demonstrates in varying degrees the changing voice and shifting position of the Anglophone Cameroonian writer today. It is from this point of view that writing in English in Cameroon will enjoy a fruitful and empowering future. This anthology is intended as a marker in its history.

References

Ambanasom, S.A. (2008). *50 Years of Anglophone Literature* (unpublished).

Boehmer, E. (2005). *Colonial And Postcolonial Literature*. Oxford: Oxford University Press.

De la Taille, G., K. Werner and V. Tarkang (1986). *Balafon*. Harlow: Longman.

Jenkins, J. (2006) *World Englishes*. London: Routledge.

Kachru, Braj B. (1982). *The Other Tongue: English Across Cultures*. Urbana: University of Illinois Press.

Kachru, Y. and C. L. Nelson (2006). *World Englishes In Asian Contexts*. Hong Kong: Hong Kong University Press.

Kalra, V. S., R. Kaur and J. Hutnyk. (2005) *Diaspora and Hybridity*. London: SAGE.

Lyonga, N., E. Breitinger and B. Butake (1993). *Anglophone Cameroon Writing* Bayreuth: Bayreuth African Studies.

Platt, J., H. Weber and M. L. Ho (1984). *The New Englishes*. London: Routledge and Kegan Paul.

Spivak, G. (1988) 'Can the Subaltern Speak', in C. Nelson and L. Grossberg (eds.), *Marxism and the Interpretation of Culture* (London: Macmillan).

Tan, P. K.W., V. B. Y. Ooi and A. K. L. Chiang (2006). World Englishes or English as a Lingua Franca? A view from the perspectives of Non-Anglo Englishes, in R. Rubdy and M Saraceni (eds.). *English In The World*. London: Continuum.

THE SPIRIT MACHINE
Ba'bila Mutia

It was the tradition in Yebila's village that by the time a boy turned thirteen he should be initiated into manhood. Long ago, before his great grandfather was born, a boy's adulthood was connected with going to war and proving his maturity in battle. Then, in his grandfather's time, a boy's initiation into adulthood used to be demonstrated through the rite of circumcision. Times had changed, but the initiation tradition remained. Yebila could not remember when or why *the gaze*, that dreadful ritual of leaving a young boy alone with a corpse the entire night until dawn, had replaced the rite of circumcision. The elders only insisted that to appreciate the essence of life, one had to come to terms with death; for life and death were twin brothers. You could not look at the face of one without looking at the face of the other. Yebila remembered when, as a boy, he underwent the ritual. The chance came with the death of his uncle, his father's half-brother. He knew his uncle quite well when he was alive. But there was a darker side to Fondiwan, the man who had just died. He lived the solitary life of a hermit and diviner with whom good and malevolent spirits interacted while the rest of the village slept in the night. It was the corpse of this mysterious man that Yebila was left to watch the whole night. Strange enough Fondiwan's corpse lay peacefully on the old bamboo bed until the first cock crow when the pale light of the kerosene lantern revealed that the head of the dead man had moved while Yebila was overtaken by a short nap on a chair. Then the muscles of the dead man's face began twitching. Was his uncle about to rise from the dead? Yebila was terrified. But he could not dare open the door and run out of the death house. His cowardice would bring dishonour to his family. He closed his eyes and only opened them when he heard the elders opening the death house at dawn.

Yebila's last child and only son, Gabuma, was past twelve and a half, getting to thirteen. Everyone in the village expected him, sooner or later, to undergo *the gaze*. But Yebila was worried. His son had a morbid fear of dead people. He provided every excuse to escape from burials and funerals in the village. Yebila shuddered to think of what would happen if the boy was forced to undergo *the gaze*. The council of elders would report to the chief that his son had run out of the death house and desecrated their tradition. His family would be humiliated. Unknown to Yebila, his son would meet a total stranger who, in an unexpected manner, would make Gabuma encounter death in an extraordinary way that would transform the boy's life forever.

Gabuma came to know Ivo with the arrival of the earth-moving machine in Mbelu, a remote village that was cut off from neighbouring towns because of its inaccessible road. It was the council of elders in the village that took the decision to ask the government to widen their road and dig a site for a new market that would attract buyers from the town to come to the village and buy its abundant produce.

One morning, a distant roar woke up the entire village in the early hours of dawn, just after the third crow. The first villagers who heard the sound took it for the distant rumbling of thunder that accompanies an approaching storm; but the emerging daylight revealed a promising dawn. The silhouettes of thatched and wooden houses that made up the village were rapidly receding to reveal a scattered array of palm, banana, mango, and plantain trees. Somewhere in the distance a dog barked briefly and a rooster crowed three times. The clock birds were also busy, awakening the rest of the village with their incessant chattering. Despite the dew-laden grass and low mist that hung over the overlying valleys, there was no sign of rain or rain clouds in the pale light of the emerging day.

The villagers gathered in small groups, talking in subdued voices. Most of the men were still clothed in their sleeping wrappers. The women stood in inquisitive clusters, speculating about the rumbling sound. The children too refused to be deprived of the excitement. They ran around in circles playing hide and seek with their friends.

Yebila slowly approached the small groups. He was in his late fifties and used a black ebony walking stick for support because of a chronic back ailment that had plagued him for years. He had large muscular arms, a wide forehead with thick bushy eyebrows and he was gradually turning grey. A young man detached himself from one of the groups and walked up to greet him.

'Did you sleep well, Pa Yebila?' he greeted.

'How could I sleep well with all this noise? Listen to all of them,' Yebila said, using his left hand in a wide, sweeping gesture. 'Men, women, even children, all talking excitedly like weaver birds.' Yebila screwed his face and spat aside. 'The sound seems to be coming beyond the hill on the road over there. Let's wait and see what it is.'

Even as Yebila spoke, something that looked like a glass and metal box emerged from the horizon. As it reached the top of the hill the villagers noticed something in the shape of a big metal pipe attached to the side of the box. The pipe increased in length as the box became more visible. It rumbled steadily as it approached the village, belching thick black smoke into the dew-laden air. The metal pipe that belched the smoke looked like a tail that was turned upwards. A sudden silence descended upon the villagers. They all stood transfixed on the spot by a mixture of curiosity and trepidation. The strange contraption appeared to lurch forward in one continuous flow of motion, without any visible sign of feet. Then, to their utter amazement, they discerned the figure of a man seated in the glass and metal box mounted on top of the rolling machine.

It was Gabuma who broke the silence that had gripped the villagers. 'It's the earth-moving machine!' he shouted in a triumphant moment of discovery. 'It's the earth-moving machine! I know it! I know it! Our teacher has shown us pictures of it in books.' He ran around, shouting out his discovery.

The machine finally came to a stop in the middle of the village. Gabuma came back just in time to see a tall thin man jump down from the machine's glass and metal box. None of the villagers had seen an earth-moving machine before. They backed up cautiously, keeping a safe distance between themselves and the man who had emerged from the machine.

The man from the machine wore dark sunglasses, a faded khaki safari suit and a pair of dirty brown sandals. A watch was loosely attached on his left wrist by a small black strap. His other hand held a brown canvas bag. There was something unusually delicate about his thinness. He had a narrow face and small dark eyes that seemed to twinkle with some hidden mischief. His features were made more prominent by a pronounced Adam's apple. The only threatening thing about his face was the huge moustache he sported. His upper lip was completely concealed by the thick black hair of the moustache. His dark eyes scanned the rugged features of the faces in front of him.

'I greet you all, people of Mbelu.' His Adam's apple rose and fell as he spoke. Everyone was silent. Each individual face in the crowd scrutinised him. 'My name is Ivo,' he went on. 'I'm from Abakwa town. Your council of elders requested for this machine to widen your road and dig a site for a new market. The machine and I are here to do the work.'

Curiosity overcame the better part of the crowd. They surrounded the earth-moving machine and began to examine it. Gabuma edged closer. What seemed to be the machine's feet were, in fact, two sets of interconnected pads which, as the machine moved, made it look like it floated on gigantic millipede legs. It carried a huge shovel in front of it and a giant fork at the back. Two pairs of stainless steel pistons caught the light of the rising sun and reflected its glaring, shimmering rays of white light in a hundred directions. Gabuma jumped up to see what was inside the glass and metal box, but there was not much he could see. There were too many adults in his way. As the villagers dispersed, Gabuma too turned round and went home.

The next day the earth-moving machine began digging the site of the new market. Groups of adult villagers and children came out to see the machine at work. First the giant fork forced its enormous teeth deep into the ground, excavating huge chunks of earth; then the gigantic shovel moved the huge mounds of soil, one at a time. In just under one hour the machine had done the work a hundred strong men in the village would have taken an entire month to do.

Most of the villagers abandoned their farm work to watch the machine at work. Some watched it for hours. Others were held spellbound by its mechanical movements for half a day. Some of them braved the hot harmattan sun and watched the machine work from dawn to dusk. Everyone in the village talked only about the machine. The small village school was virtually empty. The schoolteacher complained about the empty school.

On the third day, after the arrival of the earth-moving machine, the chief summoned a meeting of the council of elders, parents, and the schoolteacher. The meeting was held in the village community hall. Children were not allowed to enter the hall so Gabuma stood on a boulder beside a window. From this vantage point, he commanded a strategic view of the greater part of the hall.

The chief had not yet come so there was a lot of noise in the hall. Soon the chief arrived with a retinue of elders. They moved to the front of the hall and occupied the chairs that had been placed there for them. As soon as he sat down the chief coughed to clear his throat. The talking in the hall ceased abruptly.

'Fellow countrymen of Mbelu,' the chief addressed the assembly, 'you all know why we're here. Since this earth-moving machine came to Mbelu, our community has not been the same. The machine has only been here for three days but it has already caused so much strife. This is why I summoned this meeting. The single voice that distinguished our community is fading. What I hear is several voices—voices of complaint and accusation. We're here today to find a compromise to unite Mbelu into one voice again. This is the time to speak out.'

A hand went up in the crowd. It was Yebila, Gabuma's father.

One of the elders said, 'Yes, Yebila, what have you to say?'

Everyone knew him for his wit. 'Not much,' Yebila said. 'I've listened to all what the chief has said. He has spoken well. But I have one or two questions to ask the community.'

'We're listening,' the chief answered.

'Did that earth-moving machine suddenly decide on its own that it was tired of staying in the town so it will pay Mbelu a visit?' A few people in the hall laughed. Yebila peered at the assembly. There was no trace of a smile on his face. 'Was it not the council of elders that sent a request to the local government to send the machine to Mbelu?'

A chorus of 'Yes' re-echoed in the hall.

'I have nothing more to say,' Yebila concluded.

The schoolteacher stood up and raised his hand. 'Yebila is right. We all agreed to send for the machine because we want development, a new market, good roads, so that our farm produce should reach the big markets in town. We sent for the machine. Let it do its work. To send the machine back will be a slap in the face of the government that is promoting development.'

As soon as he finished speaking, Tita Sama, a cynical man in his late fifties, sprang up from his chair as if he had been stung on his buttocks by a wasp. He hushed everyone to silence before he adjusted the voluminous multicoloured attire he wore. He left his seat and walked up slowly to the front of the hall. He turned his head, glanced at the chief and council of elders before he smiled. It was a contemptuous, deprecatory smile.

'People of Mbelu,' he said as he looked at the assembly, 'I've heard a lot of things this afternoon, all of them strange things. Of course, we asked the government to send us the earth-moving machine. But did we know it will disrupt the tranquil life of our farming community?'

'No,' the people in the hall answered.

He jabbed the forefinger of his right hand in the air to punctuate his remarks. 'Did we know it would shut down the school?'

'No,' the people responded.

'Tell me something,' he carried on, 'is development such a loud noise that it's making me lose my hearing?'

'No,' the people answered.

'Has development become a monster that farts thick black fumes in our faces and tears up the soil?'

'No,' the hall roared.

Tita Sama smiled again and allowed his words to sink in. 'Of course I'm getting old and foolish, Teacher will say. I'm sure he knows more about development than I do. But I have one more thing to say. Let that monster and its master go back to Abakwa and fart themselves to death there.' A roar of laughter rippled through the hall. Tita Sama adjusted his attire again and walked slowly back to his seat.

The schoolteacher stood up. There was a look of indignation on his face. He took a deep breath and swallowed hard. 'Tita Sama has his own views, I have mine. But there's one thing I'm certain about. The earth-moving machine has not asked anybody to watch or follow it. It's not the machine's fault that we're attracted to it. It's our fault.' With that last word, he sat down.

The chief and the council of elders listened to a few more people. The community was more divided than ever. The meeting finally came to an end in the late afternoon. Gabuma jumped down from the boulder as the people started coming out of the hall. The chief and the council of elders stayed behind to make a final decision. When they trooped out of the hall some time later, everyone came to hear their final verdict. The village would suffer whatever inconveniences the presence of the earth-moving machine would cause until it finished its work and returned to Abakwa.

That night Gabuma had an unusual dream. The earth-moving machine transformed itself into a gigantic insect that was creeping upon the sleeping village. He raised an alarm trying to wake up everyone. But the village slept on, unable to wake up. Single-handedly, he made up his mind to confront the monster insect. He got a step ladder, managed to place it on the back of the enormous insect, and climbed on its back. He would ride it like a horse and steer it away from the village. Without any warning the giant insect changed into a large dragonfly and took off in the air the moment he sat on its back. For a while he seemed to be enjoying the flight. All of a sudden a gust of wind pushed him off balance and he lost his hold. He was falling, falling down, down. He woke up just before he hit the ground. He was perspiring and his heart was beating rapidly. For a long time he could not go back to sleep. It was in the early hours of the morning that he finally drifted into an uncomfortable slumber.

Ivo and the machine had been in the village for five days. The people stopped going to watch it dig up the ground. A few children went after school to wave at Ivo before they went home. One afternoon, Gabuma went to the site after school to watch the machine at work. Ivo was having a meal by the roadside. Gabuma approached him and the two of them looked at each other.

'Sit down,' Ivo invited the boy. His eyes radiated the faint shadow of a smile. Gabuma put his school bag by the road and sat down on the warm grass beside Ivo. Ivo looked at him closely. The boy was dark in complexion. He had an oval face that tapered down to a defined jaw line and an aggressive chin. His small eyes were separated by a distinct nose bridge. There was something stubborn about the boy's features.

'What's your name?' Ivo asked the boy.

'Gabuma.'

Ivo smiled and shook hands with the boy. 'Of course, you know my name, Gabuma.'

'Yes,' the boy replied, 'I remember it.'

'I saw you in the crowd the first day,' Ivo went on. 'How old are you?'

'I'll soon be thirteen.' After a brief silence the boy said, 'What are you eating?'

'Oh, some yams and *egusi* stew.'

'Did you cook them?'

'No. Once in a while some kind woman in the village brings me food.'

'Where do you live?' Gabuma continued asking Ivo.

'In a small room in a big house by the chief's palace.'

'I heard what they said in the meeting,' the boy carried on.

'The meeting?' Ivo raised his eyebrows.

'Yes,' the boy said. 'Two days ago, in the community hall. They decided that the machine should finish the job.'

Ivo smiled. 'Thank you.' He sounded unconcerned, indifferent to whether they wanted him to leave or stay. He finished eating, put the dishes aside, and wiped his hands on the grass. He stood up. The boy too stood up.

'What do you call this machine?'

'Oh,' Ivo said, 'a caterpillar. It's a caterpillar.'

'A cata what?'

'A caterpillar.'

'Like the insect?'

'Yes, they have the same name.'

'Lots of caterpillars always appear in the village during the dry season. They're small insects. Later on they transform to butterflies. But this machine is bigger than all the caterpillars put together.' Gabuma remembered his dream. He wanted to tell Ivo the dream but he changed his mind.

'Come, I'll show you,' Ivo invited the boy. They walked round to the other side of the machine. 'This is the name on the machine here. Ca-ter-pi-llar. See? It's written on its side.'

Gabuma looked at the large block of letters. 'Can I ...' he paused, 'can I climb in the box and see what's inside?'

Ivo hesitated for a moment, and then said, 'Okay, I'll show you.' He climbed and pulled up the boy after him. Gabuma sat on the seat next to him. 'This is the control room,' Ivo told the boy.

'What are all these sticks?' Gabuma was fascinated by the strange knobs.

'There're gears,' Ivo explained. Motivated by a sudden burst of inspiration, he started the machine and revved the engine. The sudden thunderous roar of the machine frightened the boy. His heart was beating wildly. Ivo showed the boy the function of each gear. One lifted and lowered the huge shovel. The other operated the giant fork, while another made the machine go forward and backward. Others made the earth-moving machine do several things.

After a while Ivo stopped the engine and he helped the boy climb down.

Gabuma was visibly exhilarated. He was breathing rapidly, catching his breath in quick successive gasps. His next question caught Ivo unawares. It wasn't the question itself but the way the boy asked it, the words he chose, that surprised Ivo.

'Who made these gears? Who created the caterpillar?'

Completely taken by surprise, Ivo said the first thing that came to his mind. 'God. God made the caterpillar. It took Him several days to put all these parts together.'

The boy was overwhelmed. There was a look of total mystification on his face. 'God? Really?'

'Yes.'

'But how ... how did God do it?'

'Spirits,' Ivo responded.

'Spirits?' the boy asked in utter amazement.

'Yes,' Ivo continued. 'God imprisoned a spirit in each part of the caterpillar to make it work and obey His will. It took a long time, but God finally finished creating the machine.'

'It's a spirit machine, then?' the boy suggested.

Ivo nodded his head. 'Yes, it's a spirit machine. That's why I wear this amulet round my neck.' Ivo reached inside the sweat-soaked T-shirt he wore and brought out a leather talisman suspended round his neck. He showed it to the boy.

Gabuma was speechless. He did not know what to say.

'The souls of the imprisoned spirits are trapped here,' Ivo went on, tapping the amulet. 'I control them now. That's why I have power over the machine. Look at it,' he told the boy, 'it's capable of crushing me to death if it had the chance.'

'Don't say such a thing,' Gabuma said.

'I once had a friend. His name was Samson. He was a big strong man. He too controlled a caterpillar.'

'Did he wear an amulet to ... to protect him from the spirits?'

'Yes, he did. But one day a terrible thing happened. He lost his amulet. The spirits wasted no time. They set themselves free and the caterpillar crushed Samson to death. By the time we pulled him from under the machine, we could not even recognise him.'

'What a terrible way to die,' the boy said. 'It's getting late. I'll go now. My parents are wondering why I'm not yet back from school.'

'I'm glad you came to see me. It's hard, working all day alone and listening only to the sound of the machine and the protest of the spirits.'

'I'm so happy," the boy confessed. 'I've never come so close to a machine like this. Thank you for showing me how it works. Maybe someday I'll control a caterpillar like this one.'

'Like me?' There was an expression of mild surprise on Ivo's face.

'Yes, like you. But I don't like those spirits trapped in the machine. They may escape one day—.'

'Not when you have an amulet round your neck.'

'Please, be careful.'

Ivo laughed. 'I'm always careful. Greet your parents for me.'

'I will. I'll come again and see you.' With that last word, he put his bag on his back and walked in the direction of the village. He had not gone quite far when he heard the sudden roar of the machine. He stopped briefly and listened. Then he smiled and walked on.

That evening after his supper, while his mother was putting firewood in the fire, Gabuma told his mother about Ivo and the spirit machine.

'You shouldn't believe him,' she mumbled.

'But mother,' Gabuma argued, 'he showed me the amulet. The spirits are really trapped in the caterpillar. That's how the machine works. Ivo has power over the spirits in the machine. He's now their master.'

'You should stop talking to that stranger,' his mother admonished him.

'Tell me about the machine,' Yebila urged his son. He had been silent all along, quietly smoking a pipe. He turned to his wife and said, 'There's nothing wrong with the boy talking to the stranger. What else did the man say about the spirits?'

Gabuma's mother stood up and left the boy and his father together.

Two days later, on Friday evening, Gabuma was alone at home when he heard shouts and cries in the vicinity of the new market where the earth-moving machine was working. His parents had gone to farm and he was alone at home. He came out of the house, stood outside, and listened for a few moments. The commotion was more audible. It was definitely coming from the direction of the site. He decided to go and find out what was going on. As soon as he came down the hill he saw a large crowd gathered at the site. The first thing that caught his attention as he got nearer the site was the audible discord of excited voices. A lot of people were talking at the same time. Boisterous exclamations of pity and a low subdued wail of feminine voices reached his ears. A sudden impulse urged him to run. He started running. When he got to the site he was out of breath. He surveyed the entire scene.

The earth-moving machine was lying on its side. It had fallen over an embankment. A group of men surrounded Ivo. He lay on a makeshift stretcher of two long bamboos, partly torn trousers, and a thick shrivelled shirt. Four young men were getting ready to lift the stretcher to their shoulders.

Gabuma rushed forward and began pushing his way through the crowd. 'Ivo! Ivo!' he shouted. 'Let me talk to him. Ivo!'

Ivo heard the boy's desperate shouts. He raised his hand in a weak gesture. 'The boy,' he whispered weakly. 'Allow him to come to me.'

The crowd gave way. Gabuma walked towards the stretcher, hypnotised by its roughness, pulled towards it by what he did not wish to see. He finally reached the dying man and looked down at his face.

Ivo rolled his eyes and looked up at the boy's countenance that appeared to hang down from the sky.

'Ivo ... Ivo.' There was a lump in his throat. He stretched his hand to touch the man.

'Don't touch him,' one of the elders said gruffly. 'His ribs are broken. His right hand too has been shattered to pieces.'

The boy's face turned pale. A choking feeling gripped his throat. Chilly fingers crawled down his spine and froze his already immobile body on the spot. 'What ... what—.'

With a great effort Ivo's lips parted. 'The spirits ... I ... somehow I ... I lost ... I lost the amulet.'

The expression on the boy's face changed to regret. 'They got you, Ivo? The spirits got you?' His eyes began swelling with tears.

A faint, agonising smile appeared on Ivo's face. 'Yes.' He uttered that single word with visible pain on his face. His chest was heaving rapidly, up and down, as he struggled for breath. He tried to say something, but the words got stuck in his throat. His bulging Adam's apple moved once as he swallowed his own spittle. Ivo raised his left hand slowly and Gabuma held it firmly with his two hands.

'They have to leave now,' one of the elders said.

'They got me,' Ivo whispered. 'The God-damned spirits. They

got—.' Before he could finish the sentence he was seized by a fit of coughing. A spurt of blood began trickling down the corner of his mouth. He gasped momentarily, took one last breath, and lay still with his mouth half-open. His open eyes stared vacuously at the pale sky.

'He's dead,' someone close by said. 'Let him go.'

'No!' Gabuma cried, clinging on the dead man's hand. 'He's not dead! I won't let him go!'

Another man took hold of Gabuma's hands and pulled them roughly apart, extricating the dead man from the boy. 'Are you deaf? He's dead! Let him go!'

'It will soon be nightfall,' Tita Sama said. 'It's too late now to carry the body to town.'

'That's true. We can't take him to town tonight,' Nwana, one of the elders who represented the chief, said.

'In that case the body can be left in the community hall tonight,' Gwaabe, another elder, suggested. 'We'll have to inform the chief. The corpse can only be taken to Abakwa in the morning.'

'Take him to the community hall then,' Tita Sama told the four young men who were getting ready to carry the stretcher.

'Make way!' someone shouted.

The crowd parted. The four men lifted the stretcher holding the dead man to their shoulders and made their way through the crowd. They walked clumsily down the road as they carried Ivo's corpse to the village community hall. The rest of the population followed behind.

Gabuma found himself alone. There were tears in his eyes. The caterpillar continued groaning and rumbling with the remnant of diesel fuel in its tank. Its tracks were still visible on the dark brown earth. They crisscrossed the earth in several directions. Gabuma walked round the caterpillar, first clockwise then anticlockwise. He looked at it with a mixture of curious fascination and fear. In its present position on the embankment, it appeared harmless, almost helpless. The boy found himself wondering whether it would ever stand upright again. Were the spirits lurking in it? Had they escaped?

He had almost made a complete circle round the machine when his attention was attracted by a piece of leather that was half hidden in a small patch of grass. The flaming redness of the sun as it set over the horizon illuminated the brown leather. It was Ivo's amulet! Gabuma was afraid. He wondered whether he should pick it up. He came closer and hesitated for a moment. He saw Ivo's agonised face again. Fragments of memories of their conversation flooded his mind. He looked at the amulet for a long time before he bent down and picked it up. There was no need for him to be afraid anymore. He passed the amulet over his head and wore it round his neck. As soon as he wore it he felt a tingling sensation inside him. Then he experienced a heightened awareness. Something in him had changed. There was an expression of firm resolve on his countenance. He turned round suddenly and began walking home. He was now ready to undergo his initiation ritual. He would tell his father this evening, after supper.

MY FIRST MILLION
Florence Ndiyah

Files piled high on my desk, some covered in layers of dust gathered through several dry seasons; but I'm idle. Discoloured, unpadded, wooden chair – can't expect better for a person in my shoes. I hate to remember but I can't forget that I've occupied this same office and this same despicable seat for a long time. Indeed, time has been the only varying factor around here. Like those yellow metal boxes on rubber wheels rolling around the city and hooting into my ears as though they were just next door, eight years have rolled by since the day I first strode into this room with its stained walls and caved-in ceiling, dirty floor and dusty desks. The strenuous journey up the multiple flights of stairs, each morning, consumes my light breakfast. A few hours in this crammed box leaves my cotton shirt soaked with sweat. I'm fifty and still fighting, still fighting even for personal space, given that my officemate readily transforms our working area into his living room. Four hours out of eight, our working language is his vernacular and our colleagues, his tribesmen who file in and out with the promptness of people respecting important appointments. I wish I could get rid of him and of this office. I wish I could move next door or to the next floor or to the next building.

If God can just give me one opportunity, make me important just for one year, I will set an example. I will bring to book all those guilty of taking the nation hostage. I will run schemes to release the potential imprisoned in the masses. I will turn shacks into skyscrapers. Just one year, God, just one year in the corridors of power, and even the beggars on the streets will know there's a man at the top.

If I return home today without money for food, just two thousand FCFA (Franc Communauté Financière Africaine), my wife will have me for dinner. And if I don't get money somehow, I'll also have to give up my car and take to zooming in those yellow boxes. I'm fifty and fighting even for a comfortable ride? If only I could turn paper into money!

Well, in the absence of a magical wand, I'll go to the Ministry of Finance and Development to follow up on the payment of office stationeries I supplied to the Ministry of Agriculture. But of what use is a trip to the Ministry of FINANCE without an envelope to slip into an expectant hand? I was hoping that some of the owners of these files on my desk would come and oil my palms so that I in turn go and oil the palms of those sitting on the treasury bond for my contract. Nobody has shown up yet, but that wouldn't stop me from trying to talk with my mouth instead of with an envelope. And who knows? I just may discover that the person with the right signature is a former classmate or a one-time friend. No one here will miss me. If someone does, my coat, which I'll hang on my chair, would give out the simple message that I'm just around the office somewhere. After all, the Ministry of Science and Technology is two blocks of five floors of hundreds of doors.

Is this how tattered this shirt really is? Without the coat to cover it, I look just like one of those blind beggar's guides. I now understand why my wife always insists that I put on a coat over this particular shirt. Several times I've promised to buy some clothes for myself, but the only thing I've ever succeeded in doing is drilling another hole in my belt. Not only am I unable to afford a new one but also, thanks to my heavy burden, I've lost the weight I flaunted when I lived on my parents' pockets. Now I look like an under-fed basketball player, my lanky frame emphasised by my round head on which suspend goggling, horn-rimmed spectacles.

Like many of my fellow civil servants, I depend mostly on my month-end pay package, which normally vanishes by mid-month because half goes to repay loans. Borrowing again becomes the next alternative to stealing. I hate to look into a mirror because the grey strands on my temple convey only one message: A woman and six children bare my name, a name that doesn't go on leave, talk less of retirement. When the wife doesn't want a new pair of shoes, one of the children wants a new uniform. Just how then can I think of clothes for myself when I'm practically limited to a hand to mouth existence? Oh, why did I opt for a career in the civil service? It's all about little money, lax supervision, and much spare time. Such are what pushed me to go around tendering for contracts through my company situated in my briefcase. In my present situation, I do what I have to in order to survive, even if it means going against the principles my parents fought hard to implant in me. If there has to be change, it has to be instigated from the top. That's exactly why I want power: to set the winds of change in motion.

12.50. I'll miss the one o'clock news if I take off now. Of all times this isn't one to miss either the one o'clock or five o'clock news bulletins, not when an anticipated cabinet reshuffle has kept the nation guessing for one week. Every new day comes with an increased probability of being the day of confirmation. Today may just be that day. If I could just be appointed a director! I know thousands of civil servants in all ministries nurture similar dreams and that less than one percent of us will live to savour fulfilment. But that can't prevent me from dreaming. Hope. That's what makes me pull the blanket off my body each morning. In my twenty year career as a civil servant, I've soared as high as a director and plummeted as low as a field worker. The curve of my professional life is now mid-way between the peak and the trough, on the way up, hopefully.

The same old stuff in the news: The Minister of this, inaugurating that; the Secretary General of this, chairing so and so meeting. And what about the news which almost makes us stick our radios to our ears? I better turn off the damn thing and concentrate on listening to the voice in my head which may come up with an excuse good enough to make my wife want to take on the risk of getting another loan for our survival.

What have I done instead? Turned up the volume? I can hear my heart throbbing as though it were inside my ears.

'...press release just coming in. According to presidential decree number two hundred and twenty, the Head of State has reshuffled the cabinet as follows ...'

The boisterous feminine laughter from next door has abruptly ceased. The ministry is suddenly still. All ministries are listening. Like me, every squatting civil servant is eager, hoping it'll be his or her turn; the upright are anxious, fearing they'd be forced to stoop.

I thought I was standing? When did I glide onto this skeleton of a chair? And I'm fanning myself with some sheets of paper? Those others scattered on the floor dropped out from one of those files as I pulled out my fan, but I just can't pick them up, not now. How I wish this were the last time I sit on this loathsome chair in this stuffed cage. What wishful thinking! The truth is that it's not so much about being appointed as it is about knowing someone who knows someone on that golden list. I might know someone and my life might change through that important someone. Through that someone I might have my opportunity to become important – to be put in charge of a budget.

'Minister of State in charge of Football Affairs: Mr Sama Max'

I hadn't realised my colleague had returned to the office. What is he doing? Punching me? Has he gone mad? Or is he trying to punch reality into me? I must be in a dream. But I can hear my mobile phone ringing and ringing. Are those my colleagues crowding at my door, each trying to wade through to me? From where could those sheets of papers on which they are trampling have come? Anyway, it doesn't matter. Men are falling into my arms like women and plastering kisses on my jaws as though I were their lover. It seems if I don't press the green button on my mobile phone to accept the incoming call, it won't stop contributing to this rowdiness.

'Tell me I heard what I thought I heard. I need to have you confirm it in order for me to believe it. I will meet you at your office. No! I'm sure you're on your way to your new office. I will meet you at your house later. Congratulations again!'

So it is true! Oh my God! I am not dreaming! Oh my God! But she said something about meeting me at my house. Yes, my house! By the time I get the chance to return there, it will be full like the football stadium when the Indomitable Lions are thrashing an opponent here at home. Those people will need to be entertained. What magic do I perform to get money to appear immediately? Of course, but I have power. I now have power and authority! I need at least two hundred thousand FCFA and in fresh banknotes. So to which of my colleagues, no, former colleagues, do I give the opportunity of becoming my errand boy? My officemate? 'Former' officemate?

'Yes, Mr Minister, anything you say.'

He's smart. He knows his only way to the top is on my coattails. Ops! I almost forgot about my wife. I have to put through a call to her before she gets another reason to show me there's a bit of man in her.

'Don't you give priority to your wife any longer? I've been trying to call you but your line has been jammed. God is really so good. My class is full of colleagues eager to congratulate me. The house will be full as well. So should I return home and wait for the money?'

What does she think? That I'll start hiring catering services immediately? Coming from the field of inhaling chalk dust and chaperoning class three pupils, she'll definitely need some classes for her new role as a minister's wife. But what about me? I will certainly need more lessons in my new role as minister than her. Yes, I am now a minister! So what happens next?

I don't remember how I managed to wriggle myself out of that office or what transpired between one and seven o'clock. All I know is that I'm now at home. Home. Every nook and cranny hosting a human form; a joyous crowd engulfing me and almost lifting me off my feet to the dismay of the powerless protocol officers; my three bedroom apartment short of space for private discussions which are now in urgent demand, thus transforming my bedroom into public space. My home! I can't believe I'm looking into the eyes of people of all calibres: personalities queuing up in an apartment they would have opted not to visit before this day; my tribesmen hailing their kinsman gone a step further; runaway relatives claiming blood is thicker than water; former friends boisterously chanting 'make new friends but keep the old; one is silver and the other is gold'; former colleagues 'showing their faces' such that they may be remembered as I appoint my collaborators or privileged when I start awarding contracts; former schoolmates singing the anthem of our alma mater. I'm not surprised my wife's friends and colleagues are here to celebrate her new status, but my children's friends and schoolmates? What could they have told their parents? Or could their parents have urged them on? Businessmen and women are making the rounds. Members of my predecessor's cabinet are doing the polite thing, hoping to lure me so I let them stay on. Power can never be sour. It is sweet, too sweet.

Three o'clock in the morning. It's no secret the only people who can still afford to hang around at such an ungodly hour are hungry relatives. In between mouthfuls of beer, I listen to them chant:

'*Ma vie a changé; mon frère est nommé.* My life has changed; my brother has been appointed.'

Today is the day I take over my new job. I need to get some rest if I want to spare myself the embarrassment of having someone jab into my ribs to drive away sleep. But let me take one more look at my former life before I drown it in sleep.

Look at that old and tired Mitsubishi in the garage under the staircase. How could I have known that driving it to work yesterday was to be the last time I clambered behind the steering wheel? I don't even know how it returned there or in which car I arrived home. All I know is that I'll be picked up in the morning in a chauffeur-driven Land Cruiser with an aide-de-camp in the front seat. Following behind will be a Peugeot 406 filled with black suits of protocol officers and bodyguards.

My life has changed! Money and power have come into my life! But I'm also aware that from this moment on, I'll have to deal with much pressure as I face the downside of possessing money and power. As soon as vultures sniff dead flesh, they spread their wings and prepare their talons for landing. I could almost hear the contractors as they dished out orders to their employees during the emergency meetings of yesterday:

'Get yourselves to the field tomorrow for the handing over ceremony. If he's been a director before, then his former top colleagues will be present. I need to know who his former bosses were. Don't come back without a copy of his CV. I need to know who sat on the same bench with him in school and who forced arithmetic into his head.

'I want to know his wife's names, maiden name especially. I want to know who calls her by her first name. I need to know who gets into her house through the back door and who opens her refrigerator. Keep your eyes open. I need to know what brand of wine she drinks or serves – that's a foolish statement since her taste buds are bound to become more refined.

'Anyway, I need you to bring back the names of those ladies who would offer invisible bouquets. Pick out those women whose eyes behold the wife with exaggerated envy. Follow the minister's eyes and see where his gaze lingers and teases. One thing is certain: They'll all be there, past and present girls. I need to know all. One way or another I need to get that contract for rehabilitating the stadium.

'You know tomorrow is the only day when protocol wouldn't be so strict, when a gift may be nothing but a gift for his achievements. Form a commission and select an appropriate gift. Wrap it up and slip my business card into it. This mission is of utmost importance, given that we know little about the guy. What I need from you are names. Gatecrash if that is what it calls for, but make sure you attend the reception at his home. Come back with the names of those who are close to his office, his home, and his heart. X you tackle the wife and Y, the man himself. Leave no stones unturned. Good luck!'

The installation is only a few hours away and the wolves on my trail only a few metres away. In a week I will have their CVs on my table and then we will see who is who.

My first week in my new life! Though I've given up my old shirts and faded coats for three piece suits, I never am forced to take in the suffocating scent of my sweat; the air conditioner is always on. With a refrigerator within arm's reach from my leather swivel chair, my throat is never parched. With a thick wool carpet covering the entire floor, I never have to hear my shoes. An office with soundproof walls and doors also makes the hooting of taxis a sound for subordinates. Such is the comfort of my new office.

The glamorous aspect aside, something is wrong with almost everything I had planned. In short, I'm not the do-gooder I had hoped to be. I try to act for the people but the other bigger people prevent me. The pattern has become a fixed one which was again repeated only this morning. Someone walks through my door with a big smile and a community-homicidal request. I resist. He tries to entice me. I'm tempted but still I resist. He walks out, phone in ear. I pick up my phone but get the busy tone. I drop the receiver. One minute later, just as I'm about to push the redial button, the phone rings. It's one of my superiors. I smile. Soon I drop the receiver with a frown. I wanted backup but I got opposition. If I resist, it's political suicide. The truth, which I've so far refused to acknowledge, is that I've got the ability to fly high; however, my wings have been tightly clipped. What does that make me? A kite which would fare better as a chick?

No denying it: The system is a kleptocracy.

'I didn't pick out the words clearly, but I'm sure you meant democracy.'

How could I think aloud on such a sensitive matter? What do I tell this fifteen-year-old now? The truth? It's the simplest.

'No, Father. I don't know what you mean by kleptocracy but ours is a democracy – a system of government of the people, by the people, for the people – DEMOCRACY.'

What I've so far seen in the corridors of power is a mockery to that definition. How can there be democracy when the Government and the people play cat and mouse? I just hope she'll have more reason to be so patriotic if and when she decides to serve this country.

'Since you are so adamant, then it's both a democracy and a kleptocracy.'

So she was still present and determined to have the last word? I wish I could borrow some of her determination. Determination! That's what I need. In five months I've attended five galas and made one trip abroad, but I'm yet to fulfil my promises to God. Now I realise that not only did I limit my timescale, but I also failed to ask God for the armour necessary to remain clean and upright in our political arena. God's doors are always open. I think it's time I visit Him. I better visit Him before He visits me with undesirable news.

The fingers on my left hand are enough to put a figure to the number of times I've approached holy ground for personal sanctification. However, five months in Government and I've spent more time in church than during the past five years. Mosques and churches, Catholic as well as Protestant, I've assessed their internal deco as part of my job description. It's either about accompanying the Prime Minister who accompanies the President during special Catholic or ecumenical events or listening to eulogies and dirges at funerals of personalities or being a witness at the weddings of fellow ministers' progeny. Enough of that! Now is time for me to seek God for me.

Not many people think of God on a Thursday evening; hence, I think it's already a blessing to be among the few present in church. I have so much to tell God that I don't even know where to begin. Since I've forgotten most of the rituals, I think following the Christians in prayers and in actions would be a good starting point.

Wrong decision! But it's too late to retreat. So just what am I to tell a priest, a priest in a confessional? Did I mumble some jargon? Sure, for he's now responding.

'God has shown you the way to His house. He welcomes you just as you are, and He is ready to grant the forgiveness you've come to get. Just try to remember that you're in church and not on a campaign podium. What God wants is that you acknowledge your sins and seek His pardon.'

What does the man think? That I'll disclose State secrets by telling him all what keeps me awake at night? Perhaps I should murmur a few rational words just to dampen his curiosity.

'Even if, as you say, Eve fell because she was tempted, she still fell. When you say the truth and know in your heart that you're saying the truth, people's opinion that you are playing politics shouldn't matter. And God would appreciate it if you leave out the blame game. Don't hide behind your position which you say makes you vulnerable to sweet talk. And also remember that God would prefer that you don't make Him such honey-coated promises.'

Does he really think I'll give him the opportunity to make easy money by selling me to the public? But can I ignore his expectant look? Okay, I'll say something really reasonable only on one condition.

'If this exchange is between you and me only, where do you keep God? Don't be afraid. I have no tape recorder and there's no journalist under my cassock. Most important, I reassure you that I've sworn an oath of secrecy as regards all what I hear here during confessions.'

So I've finally done well enough to merit penance.

'Recite three Hail Mary's, one Our Father, and one Glory be to the Father. Go and sin no more.'

Even executing the penance, simple as it is in comparison to the gravity of my sins, proves to be a difficult task. I'll try harder but I just hope I get very visible results from this humiliating experience. Next week will tell.

The past week wasn't as stressful as previous ones. Was it that visit to the church? Perhaps I should do it more often: go to church and on God's chosen day. Yes, rather than use this Sunday as my rest day, it wouldn't hurt if I strolled to church.

The few times I had made it here, I had often remained standing at the back for want of seats. But I've just arrived, midway through the mass, and I'm immediately being ushered right to the front of God's face. I feel sorry for those grumbling early-comers, but they should have known better, for even the Bible says they shouldn't take the important seats unless they want to be tossed to the back when the big man arrives. Power! I have more space than I can use, while others are standing at the back; and my two guards, who've never heard of Psalms 23, have each been offered copies of songbooks, while congregants with voices to sing are left to chew their tongues. Power! The congregation may dislike me because I make them stand, but the priest will certainly love me because I'm generous with God. And my offertory is not tainted money – but for how much longer?

Two weeks later I'm again in church, this time with a different mission. Indeed, I'm not surprised the confessor of the other evening is staring at me intently, his glasses almost dropping from his nose. The reluctant penitent of just a few weeks ago is now requesting a private confession?

'You ask me to grant you absolution for a sin you're yet to commit? If you come to God, then it's because you know that whatever it is you want to do wouldn't be pleasing to Him…'

Let him save his breath for I'm no longer with him. My mission has been accomplished. I no longer want to make honey-coated promises to God; that's why I've decided to make Him aware of my plans beforehand. Now I'm ready to face the dealings in the corridors of power like a twenty-first century son of the soil.

Yesterday, I registered another company under my son's name, and just this morning I've accepted the keys of a brand new BMW, a kickback from a contractor. In a week compatriots are going to welcome me into their homes as I lay the foundation stone for a sporting complex I know will never be completed. My face will grace their TV screens, but only the contractor, a few others and I will know that what is left of the project fund won't even be sufficient to put up the foundation of the complex. Now I'm just like one of them: currently worth hundreds of millions of hard currency – enough to sustain several generations of Samas.

As the circumference of my waist has increased, so have the number of administrative cars transporting produce from my farms and the number of houses to my name. Three of my children are studying in highly accredited universities around the globe. The last three are enrolled in secondary schools here in at home, but only those good enough for western diplomats' children. Change has come into every aspect of my life, even the most basic. I've given up L & B for Cuban cigars and I wear nothing but gold-rimmed bifocals. I can't ask for more, living in the lap of luxury as I am. I now fit the profile of a typical minister: free cash and expensive cars, several bank accounts and many more houses, and plenty of available women.

While I had been losing sleep over the uncomfortable discoveries concerning my new job, my wife had been spending every minute striding out of shops with Gucci and Guerlain shopping bags. A secondary school dropout, she's too flippant and no more knowledgeable than her fifteen-year-old offspring on political issues. That's why I've decided to choose which invitations we honour and which we ignore, much to her displeasure. What suits her most are small gatherings with no personalities, assemblies where no one inquires to know more about the woman behind my shoulders. If an important invitation falls into her hands, I do all to make sure she forgets to remind me about it. That reminds me: I've got an invitation for tomorrow evening.

Invitations, which I longed for before, have now become as common as blank sheets of paper. My property has increased, so my name has gained prominence among the masses who identify me by what I own. Some call me Patron, others Sponsor. With many galas and several trips abroad, I needed a woman who could fit the public shoe. I didn't have to look far since I had become a symbol of the three V's which women crave: *Voiture, Villa, Virement*. I've got the cars, the villas, and the cheque signature. Ladies of all ages bow at my feet, and I yield. Some call me 'Sugar Daddy' and others, 'Uncle'. I introduce some as 'Colleague' and others as 'My friend's wife'.

So which of my ladies do I choose as companion for the Saturday party? Both allies and rivals are often interested in the private life of a public man. To keep my private life out of public view and from my life partner, I've had to adopt late night calls and clandestine meetings. I love this office because it's my personal space. Here, I can make a call when I want and talk with whom I want, how I want. I better inform my Sweetie about the party tomorrow evening before one of those 'must receive' visitors is announced. My Sweetie. She's just one of many but she's my favourite. Where I expect my wife to remind me about an invitation I have no intention of honouring, I'm the one who rushes to remind her, my dear Sweetie, about a rendezvous.

Who dare burst into my office unannounced? Who else but my personal assistant? Some days she's very professional and quite indispensable, but on others, she behaves like a woman who was denied the taste of her husband the night before. She's part of my public life, and like the two other prominent women in my life, she too is bent on creating her own sphere of influence through my name, that magical word which opens doors.

I know each of my three prominent women gains favours from predators who hope to exploit their proximity to me. What I don't understand is why they fight when each has her mapped out territory. One is the queen of my house, the other, the queen of my office, and the last, my society escort. Given that my office is the hub of activity, my office queen is the most knowledgeable and my house queen, the most ignorant. My society escort would love to be more than a gypsy. I guess that's why she hardly lets go an opportunity to be noticed. All three run into each other's realms, each seeking to stamp her authority. But it's easy to calm them down. A simple cheque solves a woman's biggest problem.

Another Monday afternoon! By the time I get home the place, as has become normal during the past year, will be filled with problems waiting for me, the reliable solution. Some people just want me to root out problems from their lives. Do they really think I'm God? Well, I better catch up on the news now in order to be ready for my meeting at the ministry tomorrow morning.

The same old stuff: The Minister of this, inaugurating that, the Secretary General of this, chairing so and so meeting. What about news on the football crisis? I'll just have to tune in again at 10.00 pm or tomorrow morning.

I was going to ask the driver to turn down the volume, but what did I do instead? Asked him to turn it up!

'…press release just coming in. According to presidential decree number two hundred and twenty-five, the Head of State has reshuffled the cabinet as follows: …

Yes, the journalist has already read eight appointments, and I'm still a minister. He should be nearing the end of the list. I can't wait for him to finish. Let him read that last name so that I know I'm still a minister.

'And finally, Minister of State in charge of Football Affairs: Mr Jacque Atagana Fouda.'

What did I just ask my driver to do? Rewind the news? What's wrong with me? I hope I haven't come down with cerebral malaria. But how can I have cerebral malaria when I don't even have a fever?

Does that mean it's real? So it's real! I have been chucked out of the cabinet! The last name was my successor's name? Oh, my God! What should I do? Turn off my phone? Maybe I should return to my office or perhaps I should just go home. Why not get privacy at a hotel room? No. I think I should return to the office and grab the money I left there.

'Orders from above, Sir. You are not to set foot here until further notice. Your personal possessions will meet you at your house. No buts! An order is an order. Good bye.'

Isn't this the guard who, only this morning, had bowed to me with, 'Good morning, Your Excellency'?

I should've been glad for the title, Sir, for one of my directors – no, former directors — has just addressed me by my first name. Did my subordinates despise me so? Even if they did, couldn't he put up an act just to flatter me?

She has cheated me! The Government has cheated me. Just this morning I presided over the opening ceremony of a trans-African Football workshop due to last for one week. I made promises to some of the foreign delegates, scheduled business meetings, and was due to close the workshop. She has made a fool of me.

Can't one have privacy when one needs it? What are cars doing queued up in front of my house? They wear sorrowful faces but I can see some of their smirks. Some are even wearing black? And obviously they'll expect me to entertain them! With what money?

I can't believe I'm going to hand over all my powers to someone else today. I can't remember a worse day in my life. Won't someone elbow me to bring me back to earth? That won't happen for I'm now shaking my successor's hand. I feel like yelling but I'm smiling. Let him not think I'm smiling with him or for him. Has my desperation made me to say something stupid? Why is he throwing such words at me?

'This is the fourth time I'm doing the ministerial tour. It takes more than a smile for the camera to stay in power. If you're remembered again, give me a call and I'll show you how to maintain your hold on the reins.'

Power! So I'm really losing you? So these pecks I'm giving my successor are my last direct contact with you! I know the moment I let go of him, the cameras will let go of me. I will no longer be in the spotlight. What can I do to prolong the moment? Keep pecking him! Four! Six! Eight!

All those who had held bouquets at my installation are nowhere to be found. Look at the same contractors who had invited me to chic restaurants and offered me expensive gifts. See them and their agents shove me as they seek to uncover my successor's entourage. Divorce with power is painful, very painful.

In theory I'm expected to return to my former office and continue answering to the Government. In reality I'm too rich to return to that rat hole. I'll make a deal with my director: He deducts half of my annual alms-worth of a salary and submits a good report on my account even though I'd never show up for work. If I can't take the reins of a ministry, I can take the reins of my companies. Now is time to personally multiply my millions.

THE BETRAYAL
Mbuh Mbuh Tennu

After watching the rain for what seemed an eternity, Dr Alexander Timbong sighed heavily from the roots of his soul and came to the conclusion that he had never been more depressed in his life of fifty plus years. Dejection clawed at his heart and annulled his desires, hopes and ambitions: whatever the words meant that was *how* he felt, wretched and estranged even from his own sense of self-intimacy, now on the verge of breaking off. Yet he was suddenly inspired by this sullen counterpart to his misery, and heard his own fate, as if from the portentous lips of a pigmy, dripping into his soul from the sad drench outside.

He was sitting in his sparsely furnished Secretariat on the second floor of the Administrative Block of the Faculty, already used to the humiliating state of the cubicle, vacant and mossy. His blank stare went through the open door and denied its own vision, as the rain drained hope out of the morning sky barely minutes before his lecture with his second year Lexicology students.

The palm trees swayed before his eyes like widows in a season of mourning, and in the arena of sorrow his own heart caught the rhythmic sway in a melancholy shudder. He too felt drenched, had felt this way for so long it was useless to recall how long. Time and its cruel contingencies was also the sodden misery outside with which he sought kinship, nonetheless. A few hawks were perched precariously on the drooping branches, rising and falling to the beat of the wind-blown and rain-soaked branches.

Alex's gaze shifted to the buildings beyond the palms. Even from the distance, he could *see* through the inscrutable walls, and felt the stubborn cobwebs lacing the undusted windows; the staircases and the corridors too, covered with a layer of mud from the incessant padding of muddy feet up and down in a bored monotonous sequence; and the walls of the lecture halls covered with outdated blown-out wall maps, crumpled and undusted. The corridors – and the lecture halls when not in use – were always in darkness with only a curious shade of obscure light showing at the entrances. In his rare interludes of humour, Alex imagined zombie emissaries and their minions conferring in the dreadful shades, hooting from their substantial invisibility to ensure the eerie buzz that hung over the place like a requiem gong. At such moments, he reflected how his mind, numbed of feeling, travelled over the place like a disturbed spirit, making monotonous rounds through the wriggling corridors and counting the empty sockets with entangling webs of cables, so that even with closed eyes, now, he could still see every inch of the collapsing arena and felt nostalgia tugging at his heart. For, the things that used to be only gather moss now, a blunted vision, hollow prognostics, and hypertensive minds. It was a weary vision and Alex slowly shook his head in a final acknowledgement of denial, shattering all bonds and pledges. It was beyond him – or rather, he mused silently, and almost amused in his new faith, he was beyond it. It no longer mattered to him whether or not his colleagues laughed at his roving mind.

'A pig in its sty gets used to it, Old Boy, if it *must* survive.'

He had heard it all before, the deterministic parroting of cause and effect beyond a crass consciousness; the user's guide drills that identified blissful subservience as the magic password for the ideal slave; the tragedy of collective surrender based on the hypnotic notion that collective suffering and death never pains. That way they found satisfaction in the daily routine of a make-up life, not theirs, and laughed like happy men. They had given up themselves finally, and without knowing it, were acting from the remote controlled mechanism of the system that glorified collective sheepishness.

'Then I'm no pig!' Alex retorted bluntly, his lips curling into the semblance of a smile. How else could one be expected to quarter oneself into submission, like a sheep on the slab, sacrificed for no purpose? He still dreamt a meaningful sacrifice.

But he could not overcome his own scepticism finally, and put it to rest. And so the days had crawled on, with their activities too, in mechanical monotony, with talk of how the place used to be *the* place. But now he no longer cared in the shadow of the place, his thoughts were removed from such drugged sentimentality and heaved into a straying rush, with the falling rain, collected right into his own settled soul. He was like born again, sure of his course, beyond the cold clamour, denying the weary trappings. That was what he told himself as he stood by the roadside that morning to take a taxi.

Mimmie, his thirty-three year old secretary, was punching at her IBM machine opposite him with a dexterity that veiled her frightful instinct for vengeance. Her mind too was wandering somewhere, Alex knew, contemplating her stiffly bowed head in *bakala* plait turning in quick sharp movements to throw a glance at the manuscript, and chasing myriad strands of her endless thoughts. Somehow Alex pitied her, he descended from his own throne of sorrow to pity her, with her bowed head of submission and rattling fingers, wishing he were the only one in the bleak place to feel such suffering. For he had developed a strange capacity for absorbing misery, and even came to love it in its overflowing anticipation of his life, ever since his wife was crushed in metal eight years ago. He was now a shock absorber, he again mused – loving the expression in a comical way – and staring vaguely at the opposite wall beyond the stiff almost unmoving head of Mimmie, and had been working for only one year now in his additional headache as Department Chair. That was one way, they hoped, to rein him in, and shut his mouth for good. How could he complain again, when he now belonged, especially as a full mouth cannot talk? But of recent, an eerie feeling constantly crept over him whenever he was alone in the office, unable to work, and unwilling to concentrate. He almost screamed at such moments, even wondering at himself and his vagabond thoughts, and scared at the terrible horizons his mind could race after and never tire. His colleagues avoided him eventually and walked away in a clustered solidarity against what they jokingly called his 'jungle thoughts'. Then they'd cross the road into paradise *Chez Alice*, to reconcile and soak their souls in an oily dish of *ka'ti-ka'ti*, the chopped and spiced chicken almost swimming in palm oil, and wash life and its worries with a frozen bottle of *Jobajo*, boasting: 'I tell you, Old Boy, this country sweet, you hear na! Anybody who thinks otherwise should *waka* good, in search of his own Promise Land; but I'm fine where I am!' That was the new sense of patriotism, in which hand-to-mouth patriots became drum majors, and harped the institutionalised liturgy of *se porte bien* normalcy. Alex knew he could not follow them and croak himself hoarse, that alone was clear to him.

But it was also what he loved, this broken spirit of himself in meditation, and alienated, as if to escape from the sorry sense of his condition. The spare table of the Secretariat had become his refuge spot, and Mimmie a wonderful diversion to his intimate horrors.

II

A shadow fell across the doorway, projected by the light from the lurid corridor bulb. Mimmie looked up instinctively like a viper in the vicinity of danger and again bowed to her machine as if she had never stirred. Only her restive fingers betrayed her frustration and the machine seemed to chuckle and buzz at the same time under her mastery. Alex too dragged his eyes to the door and was confronted by a huge out-of-form beast (for that was what his mind confirmed without a shade of doubt) of about fifty-five. Alex immediately recoiled from the patronising look with its snarling smile glued to the puckered face. He looked beastly, an enemy, the ostentatious type, Alex screamed in his heart in successive denunciations, again registering the fact; he embodied the fattened maggots of bossy ostentation that he recoiled from, and must wrestle against with his last energy. How else could he be seen and described apart from how he presented himself, the authoritative stone wall he must crush or else be crushed? Yes, they were the chop-broke-potters who were balkanising the country and people on tribal instincts, but forbidding Alex from asserting himself the way he *was*! Then a piece of the face popped and a sound came out.

'Bonjour, Monsieur et Dame,' the stranger growled, surprisingly cheerful, talking from inside his stomach, throaty and swelling. Alex looked away from the condescending blot of light framing the doorway in a ghastly silhouette, wondering as he always did when so confronted, why such fellows never bother to respect the directives *in* English which he had personally supervised to be printed out for him from the computer room! He stole a glance at his own workmanship and the words stared back at him in self-embarrassment:

OFFICE OF THE VICE DEAN:
Please Address Yourself to the Secretary.
Thank You.

It was a battle line he had drawn, aesthetically coded and decorated at the borders, to voice himself, but suddenly he realised that the words, staring at him, were voiceless. And the visitor could not even see them!

'*Est-ce que je peux voir le doyen?*'

The feral voice betrayed nothing beyond the unawareness of one seeming to tread the very edge of his own pompous voidancy. He was like nothing, Alex thought, as he looked and saw only emptiness where the man stood, and screwed up his eyes again looking at him with something between a sneer and a poor smile and then, very deliberately, looked away, in final recognition of his alienated kinship. Why must he pretend what he didn't feel? But the man did not budge and so, determined to confront him if he must, Alex turned, a strange glittering look in his eyes.

'What was that?' he said blankly.

'*Quoi?*' the man said, alarmed, with fear shadowing his eyes as if he had been jabbed in his bowels.

They were both lost again, in search of a meeting point, the man crawling for meaning and Alex drifting away from the assigned, attributed semblance of it. It was not what he wanted, nor his heart acknowledged, the cultured acknowledgement of himself to understand without being understood, so he turned away again, to embrace his own tongue. If only he could torture the man too into the frustration of his own heart, victimised if he must, over the woes of wilted faith that have stubbornly refused to see his crafted words like the Annunciation, now he realised, in search of voice. The man must be deflated, bled of his peculating pomposity and ex cathedra peevishness. Alex was tired of appearances that were always phrased, even when it concerned his own Department directly, in what he now called *the other tongue*. He finally raised a loud cry during a Faculty meeting and the response had been coated in communal camaraderie and brief: he should write, for, '*Comme vous savez, l'Administration est faite par l'écrit*' – the cultured alibi to scapegoating performance in a drab of mediocrity, Alex had muttered to himself. Immediately after the meeting, however, he had 'written' a catalogue of grievances and after a week the file came back, unattended, with a yellow slip attached to it: *Veuillez-me traduire ça, svp*. And that was the end of the hide-and-seek *parapara*, and Alex's mind was made up. He was furious with his complicit naïveté in the linguistic saga in which bilingual intercourse was defined as him speaking and understanding the other tongue and then translating himself for even a shadow of official attention!

'*Excusez-moi...*' the man began to croak again anew in his over-stuffed tone, laced with the excesses of spirits, and then stopped, almost immediately, as Mimmie's hand shot out suddenly and stabbed the frosty air three times in the direction of the corridor, further down. The bull shrugged, adjusted his lapels like one of the few lucky ones who belonged, and then cleared his throat in the vain manner of a man who was lost for words, half laughing and liberated.

'*Bonne journée, mes chers!*' and then stumbled away, revealing once again the opaque beyond.

'Must you be the Jesus Christ of every bloating tick?' Alex burst out uncontrollably frustrated. 'The man was willing to stand guard the whole day, if only you let him!' he cried.

But Mimmie merely glanced at him without uttering a sound. After a few seconds, however, without pausing in her work, she said, 'You know, Sir, that we need Christ here and it doesn't help denying the fact always.'

Then she giggled freely, tickled by her own crisp thoughts, knowing how they affected what she described as his ungodly divinity. He had stopped going to church too and looked for God in the heart of man.

Yet, there was nothing to giggle about, Alex decided, crossing his legs with a knotted temperament. Church for Mimmie was the magic drug and when she was repeating her monotonous phrases to an avid ear, she felt reconciled with the world. It was as if she knew nothing else and did not care to know.

'If he were to stop in this accursed place,' he said, deliberately furious, 'Christ would never find the road to heaven again, weep as he may.' But he was furious more with himself now forever lobbying for participation in the dungeon place where hope crackles like twigs against a harmattan combustion. What now, he reflected, with such a crippler *zazou* calling on such a bleak morning and soliciting acquaintance from his tribal throne of pride! And to think of how his very vowels inflected as he sucked the sounds of his provincial mentality, puffed out of his drawling jowls like smoke, *pff-pff*, to blur his listeners. For Alex was unapologetic about the language of his upbringing, and while he hailed the heights to which it towered and had his reservations too, he dreaded the sudden summons to submission in osmotic fraternity on soiled patriotic bedrock. He longed for the shadows of his past again, as testimony to his sanity, to feel himself in speech, dignified, and not sampled from the blown-out emptiness daily clouding his vision. He felt his strength coming back, having traversed the luxurious limits of glossy acquaintances in his withdrawal from the comedy of colossal acquiescence, and he forgot bloating Pompidou. So his mind wandered again, over every minute of his prostitution with the place, having given but now refusing to give again, himself. He recalled the horrible smiles of hypocrisy, wooden and fixed at cocktail parties, responding to empty toasts; the convivial frowns of pretence, validating hopeless complacency; Judas kisses on elf lips, drawing his card for hell and groaning in a blank joy of pain; the daggers from twinkling eyes, O Brutus. And who could then ransom the dregs of hope again stirring in his heart with sluggish endeavour, from the shackles of time? He was caught in the swoon of his own faith, but convinced now that no Christ in this temple of black rock, cut and chiselled into place, could trap him into submission any more! His mind was made up like a scrolled resolution, only waiting to be posted for public consumption. So he rallied back in his confident fury, aware that he was in battle for his life; he must resurface from the sodden moment, to rescue the petition of his manhood. And when he stirred his muscles ached with subdued rage, and gripping his heart's armour as if surfaced from a swoon, he again caught the familiar rattle of the machine from across the room. He was like a man resurrected from hell and returning home for a second attempt at Paradise, almost lost along the way.

He looked outside and the rain showed no sign of abating, pouring now in thick white sheets of tropical fury, but muffled by the concrete walls and tarred roof of the enclosure. It was Noah's flood, Alex smiled, recalling the days of his Christianity, determined to drown the place – the trees, the buildings, the very air and all. It will be the best thing to happen, he pondered, if it were indeed to happen. But this time puffing man will be the serpent hissing from blown-out jowls and should not be taken on board, no! Then he, Alex, would not even worry about things that were intimate to him like the weekly meetings of *The Bangemba Historical Movement* for which he was Secretary, and phrased out petitions to the powers that be since it was no longer necessary for the revolution to be televised, or plan protest marches all over their region in denunciation of all forms of discrimination against his people who have been raped over the decades by too much talk of national unity and the glory of the fatherland. Not to talk of his miserable lectures, ah! No, he will not care whether or not the students stared at him in a blank effort unable to understand simply because the place, plaited and hemmed in rock, prevented the seeded tree of knowledge from rooting in their souls, and bloom above the funeral place. So they too become stunted, like the place.

Alex had come to dread his lectures with inexplicable weariness; they were also the admission of defeat, his own defeat. And the students always aped him like learning parrots, reluctant to reveal themselves, unwilling to stand and unveil their souls in individual dignity, within the colossal dome of black kneaded rock. It was tragedy for stupefied generations, intimidated at infancy into proud ambition. So they instead fought to cling to his own soul, denying themselves, Alex sighed, as if to escape from the scheme of frustration that was designed and raised to drill budding talent into a gaol of collective surrender. But he will not be another Jesus Christ, not he Alex Timbong, on a black Calvary if he can help it; he will not offer his chest any more for the insidious stab, every man his own cross! He was ready to save his own soul, alone, if he can, from the gross blot. And so he would slip off or step back and give the enemy the momentary illusion of victory. If only he could conjure the Flood, if only he could, this miserable morning, to wash away the blatant filth, the denuded desert of amorphous fears and hopes, then he would never again care about lectures and apes.

'Your lecture should be in less than ten minutes Sir,' Mimmie said like a clock that has suddenly been given a new surge of energy. She did not move, and echoed to him from across a great distance with the shuddering crackle of her machine. She sounded like a far away alarm clock reminding him, dragging him out of the hemisphere of isolated thoughtfulness. For she too was a victim, and chained to her work now with a religious finality.

'I'll soon be thirty-five Sir,' she once intimated to Alex, 'and in my present state, and seeing as things never change here, what better friend can I have than my machine and faith?' And she had laughed without the least shadow of suffering on her face then. And Alex had laughed too, infected by her mirth. He had urged her into confession.

'Someone can still come along, Mimmie,' he had said with a

consoling hope, picking the fallen thread of her life from where she had abandoned it two days before.

'Sure Sir, but only to disappear again because it is always too soon once you get things really started. But let's drop it Sir ... here, sign this now that you're here.'

And so their gossip session had ended, habitually, as he scratched out a scary web on the page with automated motion.

And he thought again of Mimmie, smiling to himself. At her age, she was unable to find one faithful man in the world, so she said, who would deserve her love – or what remained of it, Alex always teased, half seriously – and assure her a future. With the faith of a child believing every Christmas promise, she was taken in, and so lived every day in dreams, ever new dreams, or old dreams repeating themselves in different patterns.

'They inevitably turn out to be terrible rascals, Sir,' she confessed on some other occasion, smiling.

Alex realised he couldn't disagree without putting his own tested faith to question.

So her work became her home of escape on which she slept and weaved her dreams. Bowed over her machine and rattling the keyboard into the song of her dreams, she was always overwhelmed by the possibility of such excursions. For her dreams never ended, her life was almost one sustained sleep of dreams in which she retraced her trips to Lagos and Cotonou, her militancy in one political party or the other, her brief flirtations to the regional concerns to which Alex was now almost married, and the list went on, endlessly. The moments when she was awake, not dreaming, were just brief inconsequential interludes in her dream saga, preserving her energy for her patterns of bliss. But let her pseudo-lovers scheme to frustrate her then, let her work break her back, let them all with the whole world rage against her: it was all they were capable of doing, which was nothing, so long as she had her dreams, to be watered daily from the fountain of her soul; then she will contemplate their every shoot and await the day of blossoms, especially now that she finally found Christ, her hero!

Alex's eyes watered, fixed on Mimmie, and blurred by the intensity of the blank stare as she, lost in her dreams and unaware of the watchful world, rattled the machine as only an unconscious mind could. So he pitied her, wondering now at her boundless confidence in him, breaking professional barriers. He knew all of her past life;

she had disclosed all of it to him in the little plots and sketches of her dreams. So he never contradicted her, and she too learned to trust him so much that, as she confided in him one day, he would have no problem writing her will if she were to die suddenly, for he shall be there to give a detailed account of her estate. And yet, here she was, reminding him of *covée* time in their intellectual Kondengui where even innocence wears a crown of thorns, urging him to acknowledge slavery, his own enslavement in a place of plaited stone walls and mud and palm.

'They'll have to hang me first, Mimmie,' he whispered at last in a bitter resolution of the accumulated moment, seeming to come awake in recollection, and again reaching across the chasm, toward her. But she didn't understand him, and looked up with puzzled fright in her blinking eyes, frowning.

'Only a dog will continue here after all the treachery and bad faith, and lick its own vomit,' he went on in patient explanation, understanding the look in her eyes. 'I've told them, I'm neither a pig nor their dog, Mimmie, no more. It's finished,' he added with bitter irony.

'Then why did you make it here today?' she said bitterly, accusing him, he knew, of betrayal, about to abandon her.

'That's what I've been asking myself all morning,' he said. He paused as if in a sudden trance and then went on as calm as ever. 'It seems I'm a coward, after all, Mimmie, yet I needed courage from *this* final trip here. I had to be very sure, and now I know, and there's no turning back. I thought I could change things here and elsewhere, Mimmie; I thought, yes I thought ... but as always, I only thought.' It was a confession, but more like the prayer of intercession, long and solemn, almost boring, and inducing sleep, after which there was the dragged out *Amen*, and the congregation rose, repentant.

Mimmie again glanced up briefly and he could barely discern the shadow of a smile flitting on her lips: it was her own way of pitying him, acknowledging their mutuality in silence. His eyes lingered on her for a while, and for once he had a strong urge to disclose the last of his secrets to her. But he could not, finally, obsessed as he was by the exhilarating sense of it, the temptation after all was just a flitting weakness, he assured himself. And because he could not, Alex felt guilty; somewhere in the remotest corner of his heart, he knew he had secretly stabbed their faith in one another. So strong was it that even in her oblivious innocence, he cringed with a sense of guilt. But how could he tell her about his interview at the American Embassy later in the day, which even this soggy morning was just another illusion? He was about to cross the boundaries of his heart, whatever that would bring, and his bitterness intensified when he looked outside to see the ever maddening rain and then across the room at Mimmie, unable to burden her finally with an awful sense of absolute desertion. For she had been his last hold onto the meagre life that the place offered, and he hers, yet he was about to break her heart finally. She too belonged to another phase of his life, after the cruel, unforgiving death of the only woman he ever admired.

He blinked repeatedly to clear his miraged vision; and very reluctantly, once more, his sight wandered outside into the certainty of drenched concrete, its will a cold blot. It was exposed in a sluggish avalanche of mud, surging as if into his heart, combating the uncertainty of his very decision, and his heart stood still in the midst of the crippling phenomena. His whole consciousness was caught in the muddy flow, and he struggled against the surging compromise, feeling his way through a tremendous upheaval of bumping chaos framed in his estranged imagination. Everywhere was covered with the muddy defecation, the lawns where the grass grew in disgruntled patches, washed in mud. Alex knew then that his bitterness against everything in the defaced environment was final, he rejected it and its years and years of authoritative chauvinism, cultivated over the common dreams of a people, and planted on sacred ground with cactus fingers. Alex had been caught in the nightmare visited upon the place, over the decades, and now trembled at the fostered insult as if of his own very being. For traces of Beti ancestral rites still survived in the patches of groves along the folded ridges of the knoll, now oozing muddy rain water; it held relics of a pathless greenery in huge-trunk equatorial timber that outlived the earth-cleansing of the ice age and was later to feed Europe's eternal greed. But a day after the colonialist's contrived departure, someone had dreamed and the following day surveyors had scaled the knoll and pegged the boundaries of the nation's highest institution of learning. Lofty dreams were realised in moderate accommodation of igneous dread, and eighteen months later the inaugural ribbon in green and red and yellow had been cut by His Excellency himself, decades ago. But all that was a pathetic chronicle today, Alex reflected, as time had been allowed to breed fungi on the pearl; and neglect, like an insistent nightmare, had triumphed on the particles of the shattered dream, scattered in the grains of bad faith, lodged in the hearts of men. Words had been twisted out of meaning, and only empty sounds now echo from the hollow conclaves. Even the marks of the ostentatious flower gardens showed only the remnants of withered blossoms, dropping from stunted stems, and standing in the scattered isolation of abandonment: it was the real bloom of ruin, celebrating a legacy of neglect.

So Alex felt his bowels heave in rhythm with the sluggish froths and he felt stripped and exposed. His mind of all minds, moving over the place then like a troubled spirit of appeasement, expected to surrender to a place of stone; cut black stones having raised the buildings, marked out the shadowy overgrown parks, the lawns and the pavements, the library and offices and parking spaces, all a labyrinth of black stone, as if some black Gradgrind had risen from a sleep of conception and said, 'Let's install a citadel of stone, raised according to the pattern of our dream.' So the place had sprung up almost of its own will, unadulterated, from the regal conception, the realisation of a bad dream.

It was never to be then a fruity dream, abandoned in the mud of abortion, only confusing the inmates in monotonous drills, and now struggling to compromise his last resistance on a nasty morning, Alex thought with a shiver. But it will not succeed, it was never meant to succeed; he must triumph in the end, it was the vow of his life, and his spirits were abroad, in arms. He had been fighting the formless dread for ten years, a whole decade of a man's life, caught in the claws of rot. The best he could do, had done, was to prostitute himself in lingering moments of bossy condescension along the paths of stone and through the passages of stone, to deliver his lectures of capitulation in halls of stone, breathing urine through the smashed windows, ten years after Leeds, bursting with hopeful enthusiasm.

Thinking about it now, and especially of the fleet manner in which Time had willed its curse on him, Alex wondered how he could have given in for so long, his back so numbed where the burden stood, his palms so raw and forever chalky. For he had nearly gone to slumber as time and time passage meant very little to him then, he had nearly been hypnotised into a moribund of living passivity. That was especially true in the aftermath of Lilian's sudden death along the Bamenda-Yaoundé highway, only two years after his return to the country. He had felt mad frustration, bled of all hope and betrayed by death, unwilling to forgive life. How could he, when their three-month-old son had to be ferried to Shisong for a fostered livelihood?

III

Something cold, like a snail, Alex thought instinctively, touched his jaw and he jerked back violently. Mimmie burst out into a ringing laughter, full of life beneath her opening face, as if set off on cue. She convulsed over her machine, choked with laughter. Alex felt something like anger stir in him but it was only the result of shock. He was confused and in no mood to ask questions, so he waited for her to calm down, when she would. But one look at him plunged her back into a spasm of laughter. He must have said something unconsciously, Alex concluded, but he couldn't say what. So he instead folded his arms across his chest and fell back into his chair, frowning like the *patron*. This produced an immediate result as Mimmie promptly stopped, seeing his brow begin to gather.

'O, Sir,' she managed to say, wiping her eyes, 'you looked like one of those Old Testament prophets lost in meditation,' she said, paraphrasing his own utterances.

'I'm troubled,' he confessed; 'this place is no good for my health and I just can't be any good here no matter how much I try. How else can I tell you?' He swallowed the phlegm; he could not allow anger to breach their unworded pledge.

'I know,' she said, calm and understanding now, a mother talking to a repentant child: it always pleased her, he knew, to talk to him like that. 'But you must get over it or prepare yourself for the grave soon.' She paused a bit then added, in explanation, 'I had to use my umbrella to remind you that you're exactly six minutes behind your lectures. You'll certainly forget every worry as soon as you step into the hall, you will Sir.'

For the first time in their mutuality he regarded her coldly and knew that he could very easily hate her too. She had successfully escaped into her machine and was now urging him to do same, with his lectures, and be drugged forever. He imagined how it will feel to hate her, but knew he could never find the will. That would be the end of his own world – what remained of it now, he thought with a wry smile, regarding her. Her friendship was all that he had to live for now, apart from the love of his son that was beyond question. He had already buried both his parents and so was his own man in the whole world now. And so he embraced her friendship with wide arms, and would willingly throw away all the loves and lovers and posts that the stifling world of the campus conjured, to secure the forged relationship with Mimmie. For he was not very sure too, at times, what he wanted from her. So he instead said, 'Can we have some coffee, please?' and then hurriedly went on, not to lose the inspiration of the moment, 'I'm finally through with this place, Mimmie, I can't pretend to breathe in it any more, I can't!'

It was almost a cry. And she understood him perfectly in her heart, only slightly shocked by the sudden and devastating finality of his words. It was the confession of his heart, beyond the doubts and questions of men, and somewhere in the silence of her own heart she felt the throb, and understood. As she reached for the pot on the shelf, he rose and went out. The view across the drenched landscape caught him like a blow against his bolting imagination, and a sharp convulsive shudder ran through him like lightning. The place was completely washed out, drained of organic meaning, and he stood there breathing the exposed nudity. The rain had significantly reduced to a drizzle and like sacrificial doves daring the unknown, groups of students hurried up and down the flooded paths skipping like toads onto a hard patches or the exposed stones. They milled into the corridors with the indifference of sheep and some paused to say a barren 'Morning Prof!' to him. He responded in mechanical snorts, feeling the words fall from his lips, unurged, and no longer caring.

Gradually, after what seemed another decade, Alex felt his spirit revive once more from a forgotten strand of memory, the recollection of burning nostalgia for home some frosty winter evening at Leeds, now settled in the love of his son. It was the eddying rains, he thought, as if to banish the thought. But the feeling strayed, stubbornly refusing banishment and, in a flash, Alex was finally convinced that he could find his peace at last only far away from the muddy violation that clutched the souls of the men with a barren love. Before this moment, even the planned visit to the Embassy seemed like something that was only meant to be talked about but now, somehow, he was convinced it would come to pass. He was only a bit anxious and in this mood recalled his first interview with the white man some three decades or so before, seeking admission into Sasse College, a shy uncertain man-boy. His manchild fears and hopes returned now and the confused anxiety that crowded his mind then as his mother encouraged him to abandon all doubt at home and walk into the white man's world with courage. He felt that hope now, foolish as it may seem, and thinking of the supportive documents in his briefcase, he knew that he must leave and walk beyond the huge iron gate with smeared paint that camouflaged the entrance into the garden of mud, now drained at the base of the stone buildings, or spread over the pot-holed layer of thin tar in the yard, like the manure of desecration. He must walk off, and away, like the hero of his own heart, bearing his own cross and shield, to find his life where he must. He had even crafted another voiceless testament and must give it voice:

> staying is a death hiss;
> departure a promise.

And as he watched the exhausted showers eddy out over the fenced enclosure above which he also imagined his bannered words flying in celebration, Alex saw a last hawk rise gently on full-stretched wings and, instead of joining its kind in the rhapsody of after-rain, it circled the palm tree in a gentle unruffled sway before sweeping westward, flapping its powerful wings in flight. He sighed as if purged, following the disappearing bird with his heart, vanishing into the sunless skies. And knew finally that his thorny path of hope lay beneath his own soles and let the heavens collapse, victory was the ultimate child of the resolute heart, like his, borne over muddy cleavages in pilgrim strides.

And behind him from the doorway, like a temptress, Mimmie called out as if in a secret code that could be understood by none but the two of them, 'Your coffee, Sir.'

As he entered the office again he was thinking of the draft letter in his drawer, to be completed, signed and sealed, as testimony of the dust beaten off his feet.

KAKAMBA
John Nkemngong Nkengasong

When he drove up to the Yaoundé University Teaching Hospital that chilly Tuesday morning, he knew that he would spend very little time in consultation and return to his office where he had a number of urgent assignments to do. He had felt feverish for a couple of days and decided to seek early medical attention before matters had become worse. He had tasks to accomplish, stories to write for *The Independent Voice* newspaper of which he was editor. The paper was recently enjoying a burgeoning reputation, which had to be sustained at all costs. Above all, he had distinguished himself on the scene of pan-African thought by winning the first prize, the 20.000 dollar award for his article 'Africa Past, Present and the Future: Challenges of the 21st Century'. The Pan-African Institute which was the main sponsor was organizing an award-giving ceremony in West Africa to honour the laureates. That was the apogee of his life and he was putting every aspect of himself and effort towards the memorable event to take place in just two weeks. As he packed his car and went to the reception desk, the feverishness deepened into his being; wrecking his spirits and summoning a bitter taste into his mouth.

After paying the consultation fee he submitted his medical booklet to the nurses attending the doctor. He found a place on a bench in the consultation hall where a multitude of other patients sat, engrossed in thoughts and waiting for their turns to be called into the doctor's cabin. He folded himself up against the gusts of chilly breeze that came into the hall through an open window and the strong smell of drugs that occasionally filled the hospital vicinity, his mind fixed on the editorial he had to write before sending articles for the printing of the Wednesday issue of the journal.

It was a long time before he was called into the doctor's consultation cabin. As he entered the cabin and closed the door behind him, the lady of about forty-five sat behind a table with a stethoscope hung from her neck.

'Have a seat' she said, as she turned over the leaflets in his medical booklet.

'How's your health, Mr Kakamba?' She enquired.

'I've had fever for a couple of days,' he said.

'Nothing more?' She asked.

'Just that, Doc,' he replied. She took a thermometer, flicked it and inserted under his armpit.

'Taken any medications?' She asked.

'None, Doc,' he said. She noted details in his medical record, turned over the pages, noted details, removed the thermometer from his armpit, held it a little above her head, examined it and noted the details.

'What's your profession, Mr Kakamba?' She asked.

'Journalist with *The Independent Voice* newspaper,' he said.

'Married?' She asked. He cast a quick glance into the face of the doctor, then to the index finger of his right hand which he was gradually pulling.

'Are you married, Mr Kakamba?' asked the doctor peering into his eyes. There was a crack in her voice as she spoke.

'No, Madam,' he said, wondering what on earth his illness had to do with his being married. The doctor noted some details in his medical booklet.

'Have you done the HIV/AIDS screening test before?' She asked. Kakamba sat for a while dumbfounded, his blood seemed to congeal in his veins and he felt a dull rhythm beating in his brain.

'Done what, Madam?' he asked as if he had not heard the doctor's question.

'I'd like to know if you've done the HIV/AIDS screening test,' she repeated, emphasizing every syllable of her words. Kakamba removed a handkerchief from his trouser pocket and wiped the bubbles of sweat that settled on his forehead.

'No, Madam', he said.

'Why haven't you, Mr Kakamba?' She asked. He was quiet again.

'Why haven't you, Mr Kakamba?' she asked again, staring at him in the face.

'I've never thought about it,' he said.

'It's quite important for you to know your status, Mr Kakamba', she said. 'Would you like to do the test now?' she asked further.

Kakamba was quiet, staring into the open space of the room. He had least thought about that. And at the moment the cause of his ailment looked so sudden but so certain. He noticed that he had lost considerable amount of weight when the nurse took his weight. He remembered that not long ago, after a Christmas party, he had made love to a not-so-familiar girl without protection. He relived the whole incident in his mind and he was gripped by a moment of terror. The thought was too terrifying for him to bear and he didn't just want to think that the fever was a manifestation of what everyone dreaded most. A severe sense of guilt haunted him as the incident of unprotected love filtered into his mind. He thought he should say 'No' or just get up from the chair, open the door, step out into the hall, sneak into the corridor, rush into his car and disappear into the streets and never pass through that part of the city for the rest of his life.

'Save time, Mr Kakamba,' the doctor said severely, hitting her fist lightly on the table.

'Yes, doc,' he said, shuffling in his chair and folding his arms firmly on his chest.

'Good. What will you do if it's discovered that you're HIV-positive?' She asked, examining his countenance closely. He turned away his head and thought for a while. Kill himself? Live and die with AIDS? See all hopes and dreams crushed by one little slip of a careless life?

'I'll meet you for advice,' he told her.

'Very good. I'll prescribe you some medications for the fever. But it's also important for you to do a malaria test and also the HIV/AIDS test and meet me on Friday with the results,' she said and handed him the prescription sheet and the lab test request sheet.

Kakamba went through the corridor and turned into the reception hall of the laboratory. The smell of drugs filled his senses and the bitter taste invaded his mouth. There were a number of persons waiting in the hall. He queued up behind a couple of persons and trailed slowly until he reached the reception counter. When he submitted the lab request sheet, the man behind the counter took it, read through it and stared searchingly into his eyes.

'This, for you?' he asked.

'This is for me', Kakamba replied. There was a slight twitch on the man's lips and he could see him struggling desperately to suppress a sneering expression. The man handed him a withdrawal slip and asked him to sit on the bench. He sat on the bench unsure of what the next action would be. He was so scared asking any questions. He sat on the bench, his mind searching far and wide, from the dream to the nightmare that made him tremble.

It was not long when a lab assistant stood at another entrance of the hall and called: 'Mr Kakamba'. He rose instantly. He wondered why they were so fast in treating his case. He had become an emergency, he told himself. He followed the lady into a corridor which also served as an office. Two lab assistants in white frocks and headscarves sat round a small table. They were like two ghosts guarding the gates of death. They handed him three small bottles and directed him to the next room where his blood sample was to be taken. He passed through the door and entered into a vast corridor and headed down it.

'Not that way, the AIDS lab is to your right', shouted one of the lab assistants. Kakamba shivered with panic. The clouds were already gathered on the horizon. It was surely going to rain on him. He followed the new directives and arrived at the AIDS lab.

'Come in,' said the lab assistant, quickly wearing gloves and receiving the bottles. 'Sit down,' she said, took a syringe and extracted samples of blood in the three bottles.

'Your results on Friday', she said.

'Thank you,' he replied and left the hospital.

When he got to the office he couldn't work. His whole vision of life was shrouded in the mist of his past. He turned over the pages of his life and lamented that his state of drunkenness had pushed him that time to make love without protection. His heart ached with pain and he wished he had never gone to the hospital. He wished that Friday would never come. He wished he had never been born at all — oh! to become an object detested by mankind.

Friday did come and at 10 a.m., he showed up at the reception counter of the laboratory block in spite of himself.

'My lab results,' he said nervously to the man behind the counter, a lump crackled in his voice as he spoke and presented the withdrawal slip.

'AIDS patients receive results at the HIV/AIDS unit,' he said, handing the withdrawal slip back to him and attending to another patient. He stood for a while, then went reluctantly to the HIV/AIDS section of the laboratory where he presented his withdrawal slip. A lab assistant took it, went into an inner room and when she returned he noticed a troubled expression on her face. He felt hot blood rushing in his veins and his hair stood on end.

'Please, you'll hold on for a while. Have a seat on the bench over there,' she said again pointing to the end of the corridor where two persons sat on the bench. One of them, completely dried up like the fibres of a dead yam, leaned uneasily on the wall. His eyeballs rolled in his head like two minor spheres. It was clear that the fellow was a chronic patient whom death seemed to have rejected. Sweat poured profusely from his body and his heart beat strongly in his chest.

He heard the sharp wheeze of a door opening again and immediately, the lab assistant stepped into the corridor with a sheaf of papers in her hand. She moved towards them with quick short steps. He instantly felt an urgent need to urinate. He rose to his feet, sat down, stood up, sat down, stood up and stretched his trembling hand to receive whatever she had for him. The lady walked passed him and went towards the ghostly patient and handed an envelope, gave some instructions and then turned towards him.

'Hold on for a while,' she said and while she went into the inner room he stood waiting, waiting for life or death. She returned almost immediately.

'Your result, sir,' she said and handed a sealed envelop to him. His hands shivered as he received it, looked at the lab assistant expecting more instructions from her.

'Nothing more?' he asked hoping that she'd tell him immediately whether or not he had been programmed for death.

'Meet your doctor for advice,' she said sourly and without waiting for another question she departed. He stood for a while, wiped his face with a handkerchief several times. The lab assistant's words echoed in his mind with all the insinuations of a HIV-positive status. He turned the envelope in his hands and wanted to open it but the anxious gaze of the people in the corridor made him to change his mind. He left the scene.

He didn't go straight to his doctor as he was instructed. He wanted to see the results before meeting her. He went out of the hospital to where he had parked his car, opened it and sat inside, held the envelope and for a while did not have the courage to open it. Then he pressed the envelope between his hands, covered his eyes and cried; 'Lord! Oh Lord, let your servant die but not with the horror!' He ripped open the envelope and unfolded the paper in it. He could not immediately make sense of the many signs and abbreviations on the paper. It needed expert knowledge. He felt blood rushing through his veins and his heart pounding heavily; his hands trembled as he struggled to understand the results. He surveyed the paper over and over until he saw the word boldly printed out: 'NEGATIVE'. He ran his palm over his face several times and read through that section of the paper again and the sense became clearer now. 'HIV/AIDS: NEGATIVE'. He screamed in the car, came out of it and skipped about talking like one possessed. He hurried to the doctor and submitted the results.

'Now that you know you are HIV-negative, Mr Kakamba, it is important for you from now hence to protect yourself from getting infected. Africa needs progressive young men like you,' she said.

'Thank you, Madam. I'm so grateful, Madam,' he said.

'Good luck,' said the doctor offering Kakamba a handshake and calling in the next patient.

Out of the hospital Kakamba felt like he had been born again. He hurried into his car, revved the engine and drove into the streets, head high, his spirits beaming with life, buoyant with life. But one thing kept coming to his mind. It was a saying his mother always told him: if a snake bites you then flee next time even at the sight of the millipede.

JURY OF THE CORRUPT
Wirndzerem G. Barfee

Who is this madman frantically waving his hand up and down under the hot sun of this Yaoundé afternoon traffic? Look at him. He is virtually on the tarred way down from paved taxi-stop. That's opposite Education. His face is streaming with rivulets of hot sweat. His right arm, raised restless and waving, betrays maps of soaked armpits of his creased blue-black suit. The left hand, with a sweat-stained handkerchief that used to be white, is systematically busy wiping his ever-welling sweat-beads. Hear the man yelling: *Taxi! Taxi! Trois cents Mendong!* None of the hooting yellow cabs or their cursing drivers give him a damn. He curses: *Merde! Quel bordel ça!* A driver blasts back: *On t'a vendu au village, Vieux? Dégage-toi du goudron sinon je t'écrase à jambon!* He strikes back: *Fiche le camp! Laisse-moi les petits mots de Yaoundé là.* The driver is forced off – disappearing with his own unheard repartee – by more blaring horns from his impatient colleagues who are stringing a long train of yellow jalopies behind him. Crowds of people waiting for taxis behind the over 47 year old cab hailer, plead on the elderly man to come back up the pavement, if at all, he still loved his wife, children and grandchildren. Who cares – *Qui s'en fout!* retorts the old man. *Je bosses mon cul pour eux tous, cette putaine de famille!*

Instantly a silver Prado VX, latest coupé, cruises up to the man who's just sworn he's toiling out his ass for his godforsaken family.

—*Monsieur Dongo, bonjour!* A well fed man in black Super100 suit and vermillion silk tie bulging with a *noeud italien,* calls leaning out through the window of his hind owner-seat.

—*Bonjour Monsieur le Directeur.* Dongo greets back touching the tip of his sweat-wet hat and bowing obsequiously as he greets. He is fully conscious of the crowd and the impact that would have in inflating the Director's ego. He's surely got the director's softest spot.

—Get down Dinga and open the door for my friend, *mon très bon compagnon de route*! He calls out exuberantly to his driver. Dinga undoes his seat belt, jumps down and opens the back car door with an unwilling bow of courtesy – you can see it from his stiff neck and forged smile. He's putting up a fake face; he does not think the man fumbling now to fasten his loose and sweat-soaked tie-knot, deserves a ride in the car he drives.

—*Merci, Monsieur le Directeur.*

—*De rien, camarade.* But what has brought you to the taxi-stop under this peeling sun – *un fonctionnaire de ton état!* – You are still at the Ministry, isn't it?

—*Oui Monsieur le Directeur*, I'm still there. Ten years marking time at the same spot, treating same files, receiving same shabby treatment from my young bosses, whose big parents have phoned their way through state professional schools. Dongo reported with eyes of fire.

—Stop it *camarade*. Haven't you changed! You are very bitter and critical all the time. You blame the state. You blame statesmen. You blame the system. You blame everything and you blame everyone. Blame yourself for once!

The Director is making a joke of his poor friend's fate.

—*Avec tout le respect que je vous dois, Monsieur le Directeur*, what blame do I have ? Dongo asks, dabbing remaining droplets of sweat over his face with the handkerchief that he later spreads over his left leg to be dried by the fresh air of the VX's state of art conditioner.

The Director is having a good time with himself repeating Dongo's question aloud to himself: *Monsieur le Directeur, what blame do I have?* And then reaches his hand deep into his rich-textiled, custom-tailored suit hugging the full protuberance of his tummy. From a gold gilded case, he brings out an exotic aromatic Monte Cristo cigar. He sticks one in between his dark healthy lips, then gets it out, still unlighted, and is about to speak when Dongo asks again:

—What is my blame for serving this ungrateful Administration for twenty years — and the last ten out of these twenty without promotion? A dystopian administration where the discretionary and the arbitrary are brazenly abused and confused in matters of appointments. What is my sin in a system that's savage where it should salvage? Dongo suddenly blurts out his outrage, almost forgetting Manga's presence, recalls, then in a cowed and subdued voice mumbles: what's my crime, what's my sin? Manga pretends not to have heard all that. He is looking out and away, giving the impression of a satisfied, sophisticated guy enjoying his cigar. Allows time for his friend to recover, to heal.

The Director, later, after reasoning and perceiving tranquillity, has returned to his friend's disposition, leans towards Dongo. Dongo can smell the expensive scent of his eau de toilette. Can clearly see the tonsorial finesse of a top rate barber that fenced in what a jovial colleague of his used to call a buccal garden. How can he not also notice, from this closer range, the sartorial impeccability formed by the exquisite symmetry of the top functionary's suit, shirt and tie? This is life, this is success! Dongo says to himself seeing this representative standard and trend of life led by former classmates of the School of Public Service. He looks keenly at Manga Ataba as he berates him for *existing* in a system where he should rather *live*. Manga is telling Dongo that the *informal beats the formal* and the name of the game is 'man-know-man' – a question of *who knows you* and *who you know* not *what you know!*

—*Ah oui*, Manga continues with a proud auto-satisfactory confidence, look at me, look at where I am, I know my context and I'm connected. People will say all kinds of things about how you got what you got and how you got where you are. They will say it is because of blood connections. They will shout tribal links; then before you argue that one out, man, they will swear you sodomised your ass up the ladder. But who cares. They will be the very ones lining up around my villa every weekend to ask for favours. Ask my chauffeur. Dinga, am I not speaking the truth about the hordes?

—*C'est vrai, Chef.* The driver says, nodding, concentrating on his wheel. He wipes sweat off his neck, runs his thumb down under his seat belt and gets more comfortable.

—Yes the crowds, Manga continues, they are there all the time. I swear I know all of them who say all things they say about me. Don't ask me how; but just know, *mon cher Dongo*, some of them are still the very ones who come and betray their friends and their friends come and betray them in their own turn. But I know the set up, Dongo, I don't give a damn – so long as I pull the strings and the purse – Ha! Ha!

And that's Manga laughing, searching his tonsorial garden with his brown gold rimmed cigar which he finally dangles deftly between his lips; and he still won't light it. He nibbles the end near the gold rim, then continues:

—Then you see what I'm saying, Dongo – know your turf, *maitrisez la configuration de votre terrain*! That's all man, and you'll forget your pauper songs for good. This he concludes, searching for something in his pockets. He calls to Dinga to get him the lighter and guillotine from the dashboard drawer. Dinga gropes with the right head, handling the steering with the left, looking straight ahead and professional. He finds them and stretches them behind without looking. It's towards Dongo. He doesn't see it. He is still lost.

Manga stretches his arm across and collects the instruments. The lighter is dual shaped: a pistol on one side and a phallus on the other – all exquisitely welded into one. He triggers the miniature pistol and the end spits fire. He lights the guillotined Monte Cristo, draws a stylish smoke, and breathes out slow curls of his apparently scrumptious tobacco out of the window. He is looking at the poor faces of the trekking folks. They envy his posh car. That he can see in the misery and malice of their deep and terrible eyes. The poor, they hate the rich the same way they hate poverty – but their hatred for the rich is complicated: they are their enemy and their envy at same time. Manga is saying this to himself as if to say it is an incantation to lastingly ward off the miseries of his almost jinxed past, he obsessively mutters it in his mind all the time he sees those gaunt and haggard frames wearing worn and frayed rags over their drooped shoulders. They are carrying all sorts of burdens — some on those shoulders, some on their heads – heads that are held by shortened necks written with veins bulging under the stupendous weights they carry! He sees them trudging along and he knows where they are heading to: the mud-stick-and-plank ghettos. Manga had been there. He knows it all. But don't dare remind him of those days. Days when he had just come to the University of Yaoundé and was living with his courtesan aunt at Mokolo Elobi. Those are the pages of his life history which he had blotted out of all civilized conversation.

But that was where he had known his *bon compagnon de route*, Dongo. Dongo lived in the only cement block island in that sea of Mokolo Elobi shanties. He lived with his uncle, an *Adjudant* in the *Gendarmerie*. They rented a *studio* in the unplastered apartment building that was already occupied before completion point. It is in that house that Manga and Dongo used to study, listen to music and Sunday matches on *Sports and Music* radio and lay *quartier* girls while the bachelor uncle was away on night shifts. He also spent most of his nights with *camarade* for a reason he was ashamed to let Dongo know: that was when one of his aunt's fat-pursed clients had to pass the night. Life was such, until they finished university.

One radio announcement happened that graduation year and changed Manga's destiny for good. One minister was appointed. A man in a white Peugeot 404 called. Took them out for the wickedest boozing spree of his life. The spree only stopped with the day dawning on them at Mvog Ada. He was sleeping with a half-emptied bottle of lager cuddled in his arms. His aunt was snuggled up in the hind seat inside Jean de Dieu's arms. They were sleeping, snoring hard and deep. That was all he remembered. He was to learn from subsequent appointments that Jean de Dieu Ngonda, one of his aunt's clients, had been named the minister's very own private secretary! He had been the minister's *l'homme à tout faire,* a man much trusted by the new minister, Ndingono Motnam.

It didn't even take a month and the *concours* into the School of Public Service was launched. What specialisation do you want? That was the Ndingono's Private Secretary to Manga, who, sitting there in Jean de Dieu's newly refurbished office, could not believe what was happening to him – he was beginning to surf on a dream sea world.

—Administration, he had said timorously, afraid to pronounce Taxation which was everyone's first dream. He had wanted to give the fake impression of humility that he was not interested in the money spinning *Régies Financières.*

—*Bon.* Go to the school and get the list of documents that comprise the dossier. Take!

That was Jean de Dieu placing into Manga's moist and trembling hands, a brown envelope. He had pulled it from the drawers of his well polished mahogany table on which sat a number of incoming files to the left and outgoing ones to the right. Manga thanked his benefactor profusely. The envelope weighed! His heart was pounding with the anticipation and speculation of the amount.

—Come and see me with your documents once you are through with the compilation. Okay?

—*Oui, Monsieur le S.P.*

—Okay. See you later.

As Manga walked out, he felt the well worn heels of his dusty Docksides sink soft on the thick moquette that widened out towards the thick door foamed for sound-check, his legs still trembled with a lightness that had possessed him with the auguries of positive promises, promises that were now solidifying from figments of imagination and dreams into crystals of concrete possibilities. As he walked down towards MINPOSTEL and crossed the starfish roundabout near Education towards the giant tower of *Immeuble Ministériel No. 2,* his mind could not cease fantasizing about himself in the prestigious ENASP, as it was more popularly known by its French acronym. He saw himself in sleek suits picked from the most chic boutiques on Avenue Kennedy and Montee Ane Rouge, saw himself a prince on the monthly State bursary – the *Bravo Charlies!* And what was the icing on the cake: all those girls scrambling for him, their dream boy, a guy with a future as certain and as solid as gold. *Mon Dieu,* his life would be utterly changed! He cried from the inside of him with joy.

* * * *

Manga is still smoking his cigar leisurely, puffing the smoke luxuriously out of the air-conditioned car into the moist heat of the sun-drenched streets. Dongo leans away towards the opposite window looking out, his mind journeying into the past. A past that stretches out on a road crossed with many *carrefours* where the threads of their lives have intersected: Mokolo Elobi, Ngoa-Ekelle and ENASP – a school he got into thanks to Manga who had informed him of the *concours.* Though more brilliant than Manga who had passed in the final results emerging *major,* Dongo's name appeared but on the waiting list. His luck came in the name of a Procureurs son, Ahanga Marcel Aboe (Dongo will never forget that name!), who had passed in both Administration and the Judiciary and decided to choose the latter, thus leaving him an unexpected chance.

As the engine of the Prado idles in the *Marché* Melen's nerve-rending traffic, Dongo continues to run the reel through his mind.

He remembers how Manga had had the 12/20 obligatory pass to the second year only through back door interventions from higher quarters. At that time, Manga had become very reticent with Dongo about most of his dealings. Dongo remembers how he had put himself through an ordeal of silence just to refrain from the tempting curiosity of asking Manga, as he would have done in the past without inhibition: *man, tu as joué comment, Lucky?*

The second year came and again, Dongo remembers vividly, how the results were delayed because some three students had problems with their academic performance. They had below 12. The names were not published, but the rumour published it long before. Manga, Ahanga Marcel and one Ndi Jasmine – she rode the poshest car in school, a blue convertible Beemer. And who didn't know she was a girl friend to the ministerial big shark who threw a beach bash for her on her birthday at Kribi?

A week passed and the final graduation results came and everybody had succeeded. Manga threw an excessive party at her aunt's new villa at Santa Barbara. Dongo was there. Thanks to his presence, a fight between Laure and Melanie was nipped in the bud. Laure had given a bouquet of flowers to Manga. Melanie, who judged herself Manga's no.1, found that a provocation to war. She appeared with her gang of friends ready for a showdown. It took Dongo and a host of other invited friends intense diplomacy of appeasement of Melanie, through the distancing of Laure, before the house could party in peace till dawn.

Graduation was hardly a month old, and even before integration decisions had ever been thought of being conceived, Manga was already appointed Sub-Director in charge of Budget and Material in Jean de Dieu's ministry. He was also accredited as cashier to the imprest funds. His rise would be meteoric.

Dongo thinks all this and remembers it all. His student days friend did not last two years as sub-director and was bombarded up as the omnipotent, *ministre-bis,* the Director of General Affairs, what he presently is – the Monsieur, le Directeur who is giving him a lift in this 50.000.000frs state supplied value *ultra-luxe* car: air conditioned, with digital multi-disc player, mini-fridge surely icing a Chivas or some expensive French champagne, patent leather seats and all that brings comfort from house to car! And what has Dongo, son of Mbinzi, done in his intelligent and sacrificial life not to deserve a piece of the game? Dongo wrenches his heart with the question as the car, at last, crawls out of the Melen traffic and purrs towards Obili Carrefour. The refined sound of the Prado reminds Dongo, with contrasting twinge, of his Lada. It is caked in rust at a *Niba-Garage.* It is there suffering from out-of-stock parts and owner's lack of means to command them. The eighteen year-old car is the first and the last he had been able to buy since he started work. He had bought it second hand from Mr Lushkov who was returning home. He had known the guy through Jeanine, an ex-girl of Dongo's whom

Lushkov left behind with a baby boy, Pushkin. Dongo still sees Jeanine once in a while at her *Pharmacie Alexandre*. He forgave her long and easily: he later understood the role played by the girl in the Lada's procurement.

—*Camarade*, you've been lost in silence all this while. What's eating you up? Manga breaks the silence.

—*Là ou je me trouves, Directeur,* I swear I'm in deep shit, Dongo said after reflecting a while. Since I am not a cursed country, but a cursed man, a man without any niggard material decency and dignity, an economic shoe rag! You can as well tag me a HIPP — a Heavily Indebted Poor Person!

Manga laughs heartily at his friend's self-mockery before insisting:

—But you have friends, you have classmates, you've us – what else are we for? What's the *solidarité de la promotion, solidarité du corps,* what's all that for? It's to help one another.

—But it's not easy being the one who's always being helped. It's hard playing the pariah all the time. By taking so much and taking it always, you lose something deep, and you go on losing it irretrievably.

—I understand, but we must pull *promotionnaires* up. It's a moral obligation.

—*A moral obligation.* Dongo repeats the words to himself and then says: Yes, but something still echoes wrong somewhere about it all. I should say…

—Well, where are you heading to right now? Home? Manga asks, cutting short Dongo's argument as if to prove its impertinence to him.

—Yes. I had an appointment with a customer who collects eggs from my small poultry.

—You keep poultry?

—A very small one. A delicate investment, I must confess.

—How long have you been into it?

—Getting to two years.

—Breaking even?

—Been lucky so far, though the margin is too small.

—You have the appointment at what time.

—At 3pm. That's why I was frantically hailing taxis. A question of getting there on time. But I guess I'm already twenty minutes late.

—Well, no trouble.

—What could you possibly mean by 'no trouble' *Monsieur le*

Directeur?

—I've got an interesting proposition.

—Yes.

—Knowing the kind of person you are, the personality that you have and the connections I have – Ehm…before I propose what I've got in mind, is the Anti-Corruption Unit already set up in your ministry.

—I heard talks they are about setting it up.

—*Ça tombe bien.* Then chances are…Dinga please, look for a space and clear. We want to discuss some serious issues.

The driver drives up towards IRIC, the loud and repeated clangour of hammers on panel beaten car bodies signal men at work: men and boys – apprentices for sure – clad in motor oil dirtied wear, and standing in a pool of mostly hollowed-out car carcasses, wielding hammers and spanners. Connoisseurs of sorts of automobiles, they stop their occupation for a while, look up and, severally, whistle and exclaim with admiration and wonder: *Kom c' nyanga cet animal! C' pas le Dubai gars, c' le popo! Fer argenté, fer rutilant! C' kel ministr d Popol mem la?* A few meters from the mechanics, he clears right and kills his engine.

—Okay, you can go down and have a walk, Dinga. But you don't stray far away. You hear?

—*Entendu*, Boss, the driver answers as he undoes his safety belt and climbs down. He closes the car door and straightens his arms, neck and torso. He disappears towards the garage that he's just driven past.

When he gets out of hearing range, Manga comes back to his proposition:

—Yes, as I was saying, what about being a member of the unit?

Dongo thinks for a while and says:

—Do I have a choice? I don't know the answer to your question.

Manga caught the joke's possessive tail:

—But if you are interested then I will put my contacts to work.

—What comes with all that?

—Sitting allowances, political and administrative contacts…and you expect me to tell the rest?

—Why not, *camarade?* Donga says getting arrested.

—Well, you know every hand is stained and when you will raise your brow and threaten to raise your voice they will settle your Unit guys with your part of the booty. An affair of poorly executed contracts that leave booty of 10 bricks. You guys may pull off 30 percent quiet! So how do you see that? You want me to give you the line?

Dongo's mind is now thrown into a violent conflict between his long built morality and his long raging poverty. The two had long coexisted with a peace of sorts, but now he is being tempted to bedfellow with one against the other. He has nothing to say, nothing to decide.

That is the meaning Manga reads from Dongo's silence as he asks him again if he is ready to work with the Unit. Manga phones the driver. He comes in and gets himself ready.

—We'll drop my *camarade* at his place.

—Ain't we passing by the school to take Jonas and Frank?

—What do you say, *camarade?* A quick stop at my children's school to pick them up?

—*Pas de problème.* Dongo replies distantly and absently. His mind is far more between money and morality.

Then the driver kicks the engine of the VX and it starts at a go without an argument. Dongo thinks of the tedious arguments and punches he usually trades with age-subdued Lada and Manga's proposal becomes more and more *alléchante.*

They arrive at St Francis Bilingual Primary and Secondary School. It is a fenced, L-formed, three story building painted in sky-blue and white. The wide flung metal gates reveal well trimmed green lawns whose surface is marked with flowered patterns of the school's SFBPS initials. A fleet of expensive cars is parked alongside taxis hired by parents whose other preoccupations can't make their own private cars available for this mini-exhibition, an exhibition that awaits the well fed and well taught kids who are now swarming out in their white and sky-blue uniforms. The chattering voices and back-sacks stuffed full with school needs tell Dongo the rift between them and his own children: remember the eternal complaints of this or that yet unbought text book or instrument! Remember the humiliation of unavailable taxi fare during the month's *twenty-hungry?* And the shortage of their lunch coins, remember?

Dongo remembers and swears a jinx is on him. He is deeply tempted to trust that superstition at times. *If not why can't my own children be amongst this lot?* Most of his *promotionnaires'* children are here or in some of the other choicest bilingual schools around town, and very articulate in English and French, like these ones streaming out of St Francis, without the least accent. He looks around and all the C.A. number plates confirm him the fact. The thought of his children's education aches him bad, especially in what concerns English. They only attend cheap public schools where teachers' absences are chronic. Once he had hired an unemployed English graduate to ram some of that language into his children's brains, but in spite of the young graduate's assiduity, the whole linguistic effort was met with what he personally defined as his children's 'inveterate animosity' towards the language. He announced an end to all that. The teacher shrugged his shoulders with disappointment and despair, and as for the children, they celebrated! Dongo blamed the foundations, blamed the system and blamed everything else; then cursed the children telling they will learn too hard too late... *And you will cry me!*

Now that he hears this chirping brood so full of promise, a tide of envy and jealousy wells up him. The system has not treated him fairly, he curses. His own system is raging with revolt. He has got to get rid of this morality thing and get ahead with his life, he urges himself. Soon he will hit 48, and if things don't change then retirement is mounting a *guet-apens* on him when negotiates bend 55! And who knows the miseries of pension better than him who has worked here in the Central Services his entire career? He had to act fast and stop his conscience racking his nous! He wasn't going to keep on being a Carthaginian in Rome and a Jew in Arabia! Dongo is revolting, rebelling against his past. He had to in order to live his present and build his future. This he convinced himself. And with this conviction, he turns to Manga who has just finished talking into his Nokia and is clapping it close:

—*Camarade*, Dongo says, dropping obsequious manners, see your contact and act.

—I'm just from talking to the person in charge of recruitment of members into the Unit.

—What does he say?

—We are close and it will not be that tricky. But the guy has got a condition. He'll have to scatter a million about in order to influence the situation.

—*Quoi?* A million?

—*Tu parles quoi?* What's a million when by the end of the year your own catch will multiply that by five!

—You're sure? Dongo asks with a whetted appetite.

—Sure as pigs and fats.

They laugh that one out, and Dongo proposes:

—Then you will give me time to scout for the funds.

—If it falls, I will shore up.

—Thanks, *camarade.*

—It's my moral obligation.

Jonas and Frank are arriving with Dinga, who had waded through the fleet of cars to fetch them in the school compound. As Jonas opens the front door to enter with his junior brother, Dinga takes their heavy school bags to the car booth.

—Good day papa, *bonjour Monsieur!* The children greet as they climb into the car. The father and his *Monsieur* Dongo greet back. The father asks about school and Dongo asks them their respective classes.

—*Je suis en* Form One. Jonas says.

—*Et moi je suis en* Class Seven, *je vais composer le* First School *cette année.* Frank says in his own turn.

—They are all doing the Anglophone system. That is their father specifying proudly as the driver steams the car into motion.

* * * *

Dongo has racked his brain all night long thinking of how he is going to raise the one million. The one million key out of the penury and misery that has gnawed his life materially rotten all these years, while his friends and mates cruised the fast and flashy lane. He lies by Julie's side wide awake with no grain of sleep over his eyes. In the dimmed bedside lamplight with which he used to read his old Bible in trying moments as these, he is staring at the old dirty-white ceiling stained brown with amorphous maps that betray leaking spots. He has always read them as maps of his fate. He remembers as in the rainy seasons, he and Julie had had to wake up and change the bed's positions several times to avoid waking up on a soaked mattress. Sleepless nights, such were. He looks at his sleeping wife, facing the wall, head placed on her hand and legs curled – a worn out body wrapped in the frayed lace of her old night gown. The old girl has persevered too long, he thinks to himself. She is brave. She has kept it long enough without a disappointment, a disaster. Bright with diplomas, dull with destiny. Dongo has to break the jinx and offer his family a new light, a new hope. He has to do something. Who can he meet, get a million and free his family from leaking roofs, cracked walls, creaking doors, sunken chairs, rags and bad schools! Free them from Landlords' constant and legitimate humiliations – he had changed three houses in the last six years, and had changed them down notches that marked falling standards. And his mates are moving up into suburban villas at Santa Barbara, Kuwait City, Odza, Olembe…. He looks at his wife once more. She draws a long breath, and then turns in her sleep and lays her head on the other arm. When you lie on an arm for too long and it begins to ache, it is time to change and lie on the other. Dongo remembered the proverb.

He turns restlessly in the threadbare bed sheets that reek with week-long sweat, then thinks about his resources: his bank account at Caisse Populaire is almost barren; he has just managed to pay his overdraft last two months. At the *Tontine des Frères Serieux*, he already ate his turn last December and is now on reimbursement row. What about putting an *à vendre* tag on the jalopy? Who is going to throw down even a cowry for that *Scrap-Cameroon-Unltd?* That's what *Dongo* himself call the *jap* after a swell shag! What about running it *clando* wholesale as he has sometimes, in spite himself, taxied the scrap, after office work, during the elastic months of the interminable *twenty-hungry?* And how Julie hates that shame, when he picks her up and then fills the remaining Lada seats with strangers for a fare! What about Julie herself? What can she save as a typist and secretary at the floundering F&G Business Consultancy firm downtown? How many dime crumbs can she glean from the chips and *folere* she places at the cybers and petty shops around? Just enough for her hearth!

He is just deciding on not bothering Julie when what seems to be ultimate solution dawns, like lightning, on him. It flashes like an epiphany. And why was he really scratching himself with sticks when he had knives! Proverbially, he curses himself happily. How can he forget Tamba, the moneylender? Tamba himself had approached him once about a year or two ago, to propose his usury services. But then he had enough problems keeping faithful settlements with his bank overdrafts and Tontines, to embroil himself in other high interest loans. Now he needs Tamba – 25% high interest or no, he has to meet Tamba first thing tomorrow dawn. He will be armed with a copy of his pay voucher, a certificate of non-indebtedness to his bank, a 1.250.000 Francs cheque with Tamba as beneficiary, and a ten month Standing Order of 125.000/mth – and the deal will be as good as struck! What is he groping for again! Things won't complicate. Tamba knows him well and he knows Tamba well. They were at ENASP at the same time. Tamba did the Judiciary and was now a magistrate in one of the courts around town? He is well known in the judiciary circle. He's got good money: he runs a vast, high-bonused drink distribution service in his wife's name and wins public contracts with his AB-MAT SERVICES, a screen company established in his junior brother's name. But read the company's name anagrammatically and you know who is behind it. That's what's related by his enemies, rather what he himself dismisses as the jealous and envious. Because Tamba is a generous guy, helpful and without the ruthlessness that most usurers are associated with. Gentle shylock Tamba. He has more friends than enemies. Because he is shrewd at choosing his debtors. He singles out civil servants and the uniformed guys – their collateral is egg-sure. They've got sound and steady salaries. Their cheques flow. Hardly a problem with anyone. A blank cheque is never his worry. You can understand. He will receive Dongo the next morning. And our good friend Dongo falls among the good ilk of clients: *Chef de Service,* sound morality, some acceptable self-respect and what more? He is a long time *connaissance.*

* * * *

Manga is counting the newly printed wads of 10.000francs notes drawn out in banded bundles of tens from the brown khaki envelop. He takes one of the brand new wads close to his nostrils, scents it with tender relish and murmurs languorously: Boy oh boy, sweet is the scent of mint! He smiles at Dongo. Then pulls one note, lifts it up against the luminosity of his office lamp, scrutinizes the watermark and nods: Good! He is now counting ten times ten those wads.

    —*C'est bon.* It's a million. Consider yourself a member of the Anti-Corruption Unit already, *camarade!* Manga says, beaming with another smile, deeply satisfied with the fundraising effort of his friend. He swivels round on his *fauteuil-directeur, roulant-tourmant,* and lodges the wad-padded envelope in one of the drawers of his table that holds a flat-screen computer, fixed phones, fax machine and a national flag standing, with drooped colours, between stacks of files. With his gold-ringed and very hygienic fingers, keyboarding, he raps some quick bars of music on his office table. It is a wide white Formica-ed, stainless steel rimmed, imported hard wood table. Its semi-circular shape apparently seems both to hem him in and distance him protectively from visitors and users. Above his black leather, high backed swivel chair is the large framed photograph of the Head of State observing his office and its businesses.

—So when should I expect to hear from you, Dongo asks.

—Soon as I hand him the envelope. That's next Monday. I'll phone you… what's your number again? Manga asks as he unpegs a gold ballpoint from the pocket of an immaculate white suit.

—My *portable* misbehaves. It's got some problems now for the past couple of weeks.

Manga pulls five clean ten thousand notes and hands them to Dongo:

—Get a manageable phone with that.

—Thank you, *camarade*.

—I will call you.

—Ok, I'm all ears next Monday. Dongo says as he stands up to leave the well air-conditioned and deodorised office, so fresh. Its lighting is appropriately filtered, so cool. To top it all, the Municipal Lake from that fifth floor composes a very enchanting vista, so refreshing. Dongo thinks of no better environment to serve the state than this.

—Have faith. *Fait quoi-fait quoi*, you will have the box! Manga assured.

—*Bon, on fait comme ca!*

—*Nous sommes ensemble!* Manga greets back with same valedictory camaraderie.

As Dongo disappears, Manga dials some numbers and holds the cell phone in those his conspicuously gold-ringed fingers and speaks into the set:

—*Ouais, Chef de Cellule*, how is work this week?

—*Fatiguante, la semaine*; I'm still trying to constitute the Unit as I told you last time. That is the voice of Manga's interlocutor.

—I'm calling you precisely about the name I forwarded to you, *Chef*.

—You mean Dongo Frédéric?

—Yes, *Chef*.

—We undertook his *enquète de moralité* and I tell you, the guy fits in perfectly with the kind of persons were looking for to combat this endemic virus of corruption in this country of ours…

—I told you I had a man I trusted and a man I knew you wouldn't fail to recognise his real worth and trust if you came to know him, Manga says, excitedly.

—I'm very thankful for your proposal. That's the concern all of us must manifest in this collective war.

—You can count on me, *Chef!*

They exchange greetings and Manga claps close the phone, an elated man. He has just pulled a fast one. A clean, cool brick from Dongo. He's damn right when he claims at times that his gold-ringed fingers are tinged with Midas' touch. He is right as mammon. Look at how the guy's hit a smooth, straight *baton* in no time. With no stress. Easy. Some people are simply born like that; his friends sometimes concede him that fact: Manga the Alchemist!

* * * *

And Dongo's name did come up in the Prime Minister's appointments. He was a member of his ministry's Anti-Corruption Unit. He worked there actively and diligently, giving ideas and conceiving anti-corruption slogans whose messages were printed, painted and posted on the ministry's corridors, staircases and even offices. Banners were produced and media interventions were made. Seminars and workshops in the external services were animated focusing on the fight against corruption. Mr Ousmane Maidoki – head of the anti-corruption unit and the man who had appreciated Manga for his resourceful proposal – had taken impressive note of Dongo's instrumental and committed attachment to the anti-corruption fight. This Mr Maidoki was a greying man in his mid-fifties, a *Commis de L'Etat* in the real sense of the word, a man of great integrity and open-mindedness. As head of the anti-corruption unit, he was a round peg in a round hole. He had never failed at any moment to express his appreciation and encouragement to Dongo whom he had came to love like a junior brother.

But Dongo was already becoming impatient. He had been giving the best of himself all these past months – it was already six months after the commencement of the execution of the budget. Manga had told him that that was when the *contentieux* will begin to crop up and then interventions will begin to yield returns. He called up Manga. The line was busy. He tried the second time and got *camarade* Manga.

—Yes, *camarade*, it's your man Dongo

—Oh my man! How are things moving? Manga asked anticipating some good news from his friends.

—Things are marking time. I'm sweeping the church. Dongo replied with a dark ring of disappointment.

—And what's the pope saying? Manga tries to lively him up.

—He is waiting for God.

—What's happening?

—Nothing's happening instead. All supplies are regular. No reports. No deals. No litigations.

—How come?. Has a new race of Cameroonians been bred?

—No man. The talk amongst my *gestionaires, prestateurs*, accountants and financial controllers are all scared about the newly sworn *Chambre des Comptes*, the CONAC and the ANIF people…all that pack is noisily sniffing around. Everybody's scared. And the new minister is scared of his own head too. You know he is not from the *pays organisateur*, so he fears his head the more. Nothing's happening, man. I'm dead.

—What do you mean as dead? Your records are still clean. What's the dead thing about?

—I borrowed that million from the usurer.

—You did what?

—*Camarade*, I'm in deep shit, *Je suis dans une merde totale, camarade!*

—Who lent you the money?

—Tamba, our man. Signed I will repay him in three months. Signed him cheques as collateral. Three months passed and I asked a moratorium. He extended another three. Now it is running out fast and if he cashes the cheques, I'm dead with the family! Especially now that I am in a new and more expensive house, and bills skyrocketing, and the Lada up and consuming. Man, I'm…

The phone stopped. Dongo looked at it. Pressed #123# and available airtime units read zero. By this time Manga was already calling back.

—Yes, *camarade*, the line went off.

—So I realized.

—As I was saying, I'm dead. I can't disappoint Tamba again. The standing orders are there for him to cash by the tenth month if I fail.

Manga listened and after a moment of grave silence said:

—You see, *camarade*, it's left for you to work things out now the way you best can. I have given you the wife; you can't expect the bed from me again.

—So what do we really say now? Dongo spoke desperately into the phone.

—I guess we should say that we will meet over a drink and talk about something else for once, Dongo.

Dongo hears his name fading in the waves and wiping out with a final sanction from Manga's thumb on the red stop button. He feels his whole frame go loose and limp, as if all the bolts that riveted them have been unfastened. His mind sails adrift as he sits lost in his Lada that was parked under the shade of the eucalyptus trees that lined the back of his ministerial building. A brown dead leaf falls, reeling slowly, from a dry twig. Time passes. He hears the soft noise of a dry twig fall on his car roof. Then bounces from the roof onto the bonnet and lies there still and leafless. It is time to go home.

* * * *

His phone rings. He feels the vibration of the set against his left rib. He is afraid to reach for the phone. It must be Tamba. Without a mistake, it must be him. The die is cast and his time is up. He must pay his dues. Tamba wants his money now. It's a day past. No, it's two days after the appointed deadline. The phone rings insistently and the vibration is like seismic when coupled with the aggravated pounding of his heart on the inside of that very left cage. He must reach for the phone. *Dad, answer your call!* He heard the distant voice of his little daughter calling. He pulls his Lada to a stop, on the busy road that runs around the Municipal Lake. Before the engine dies down, the phone stops ringing. He leans forward with his two hands on the steering wheel and heaves an *ouhf!* of relief. Before his peace could last, the terrible thing begins to ring again. He must take it. A man must face his destiny. He must answer his call. He takes a long breath. Musters courage. Reaches his right hand inside his coat pocket, pulls out the phone and takes it towards his twitching ear and without daring to look at number on its screen;

—*Bonjour*, this is Dongo, *à qui ai-je l'honneur?* He asks very formally.

—*Merci*, Monsieur Dongo, it's Mr Ousmane Maidoki. I've been struggling to get you. Your phone was ringing but I couldn't get you.

—True, *Chef*, I was driving and couldn't pick the call. says Dongo, relieved.

—You are a good roadsman then. Some of us always neglect the rules. I've always got much to learn from you!

They laugh at the compliments.

—Back to the reason of my call. In fact I have been contacted to forward a name and recommendation for the President of the jury of a national arts competition. A five million Francs gross cash prize for all the first three winners and runners-up.

—Yes, answers Dongo, keenly.

—It's a serious competition themed around the ANTI-CORRUPTION WAR.

—I can understand.

—So I've been asked to look for a person of outstanding integrity and one full of a high sense of patriotism.

—Yes, Chef.

—And I've worked with you all this while and I've seen, without any fear of contradiction, that you are the one person I can entrust with that task. All fairness and objectivity considered.

—Thanks for the confidence, *Chef.* Dongo muttered with a mixture of excitement and disbelief at what was rearing his way. But this trust could be hooked to the one million he paid. Maybe he is trusted because they are now sure he can play their game. He tried to speculate.

—So I'm calling to request your consent, before I forward your name.

—I'm simply humbled, *Chef,* by the degree of confidence bestowed on me. Dongo said, trying his judicious best to betray no emotions that are more than necessary.

—And I hope, continued Mr Maidoki, that you will employ the artistic genius you demonstrated at the Unit. Your exceptional ability in the conception of slogans and paintings, that I personally appreciated, will naturally prove an additional resource in the execution of your task. That's if my strong and favourable recommendation gets you up that jury – anyway I'm damn sure, that coming from me, it will be given due consideration.

The phone conversation ends with Dongo still succeeding to restrain himself from fawning outpourings of gratitude 'for the confidence bestowed on him'. He sits in his Lada and feels his engine guzzling fuel and fire, turn to another craft, his boat sails gathering winds. Then more winds gathered under his wings. An aircraft at this second transformation. He believes he can fly again. Drift in a high sky without rain. He is now a light man. Positively.

* * * *

Dongo drives around town without destination. Everywhere is good to go to. He races from Lakeside, passing, without noticing anymore, the ragged fishermen casting tattered and grimy nets into the weed-filled sewaged lake. He swerves round towards Education. Then to Bois de Warda with its green, clear and clean vegetation inspiring him as he shoots towards Tsinga. Reaching for Carrefour Golf, he sees the golf lawns of Mont Febe weave up their own lushness towards the prestigious hotel. The plush spectacle instils in him a self-sworn promise of learning golf one of these days. A second thought, an aged voice sounding like his dead father's, counsels him to desist from fantasizing such inordinate dreams. He turns away from Febe and drives his car in the direction of *Palais des Congrès*. He winds his way uphill towards the boxed-up glass and concrete of communist China architecture that housed multiple conference halls within its regular geometric edges. He gets to the edifice the Chinese capped on the top of that isolated mound of jutting rock. He climbs out of his car to view the city. Up there he can see the best of Yaoundé sprawled around his feet and over seven more hills. He sees it and starts to believe he can also possess a chunk of it – if and only if his luck sticks to the present streak: *President of a Five Million Francs Jury!* You hear that! And mark you it is *National*, he reminds the world as he turns the possibilities excitedly in his mind. The *gombo* is there! He can't just miss this one, not this time around!

From the *Palais des Congrès* hill, the evening is already falling on the city, and the mundane constellation of multicolour city lights begins to blossom over the seven low hills. Dongo gets into his car with a new puzzle clouding his mind: how is he going to pay off his debt from his five million jackpot? A flurry of ideas crowd his mind. None is lucid. They are ideas that need more than the mere flourish of a fluorescent galaxy to elucidate. *La nuit porte conseil,* he advises himself and drives off home.

* * * *

After taking his mind excessively to task, in an attempt to find solutions to the five million francs puzzle, an idea occurs to him. *EUREKA!* He could write a poem. O Yes, write a poem. Find a neutral entrant. Enter it in his name. And twist the final result in the poem's favour! *Génial!* That will be the three million first prize clearly in his possession. He will give the proxy poet five hundred thousand for his troubles and pocket the remaining two-point-five million. That will be a fat clean deal. And I could throw Tamba his one million and stroll away one-point-five thick! Dongo concludes.

Dongo jumps out of bed. His wife is rudely awoken by his abrupt jump and by the light he switches on.

—What's it Frédéric? Julie asks.

—Get back to sleep Julie, there is something I want to put down in writing.

—What's it?

—You'll know when the ripe time comes. Sleep woman. Your troubles may be over soon!

—Don't rouse dreams you can't fulfill. The wife says sleepily.

—Just sleep, wake up, wait and see! Dongo says, taking paper, notebook and pen from his suitcase stuffed with documents. His hands agitate wildly with excitement.

—You know I don't easily sleep with full lights on.

—Don't worry Julie; I'm going to work in the parlour.

He takes the A4 papers, pen and notebook, switches off the light and goes to the parlour. He sits on the long wooden dinning table surrounded by five other dining chairs and starts the first draft.

Dongo finishes the marathon draft. It is driven by the lucre-fuelled pistons of his imagination. He takes the draft up, holds the papers on the edges with his two hands and reads it aloud to himself. He is surprised by the sudden inspiration and what it has produced. He reads it low:

> O Cameroon, thou art the wide blue sea
> On which our loftiest hopes pacifically sail
> And no corrupt craft shall our horizons see,
> See none defile the waters of our sacred grail.
> Beloved country, thou art the river
> By whose water our cherished fertility depends
> And no corrupt seed we'll let grow ever
> 'Cos only bad weed'll be harvested by our hands.
> Land of the rising sun, land of our birth!
> What shall we ever know as shield again
> If we spoil and despoil to ruin this blessed earth?
> What faith will to these fields usher rain?
> And the burden of misery on unsinned progenies:

> Meditate, citizens, centuries of unpardonable agonies
> Our corrupt generations will visit on their innocence
> Contemplate, brethren, our unbridled greed's incense.

He loves it. It sounds good to his ears, especially its rhymed, declaimable, grave anti-corruption patriotism. Archaic language, he tells himself, sounds more serious and solemn to him than contemporary speech. No wonder, he concludes, that's why most serious Bibles used by the traditional churches have maintained that form of language! After reading the poem twice he decides that he will let it stand as it is. He will be more sincere. More thinking could hurt its basic inspiration and honesty, its epiphany! That is what he tells himself. He will have it typed tomorrow and call up, Ekanga, the young student activist friend of his. He will discuss the deal with him.

Ekanga alias 'Guevera' is a radical opportunist who had once, after some bottles, summarily confessed to Dongo that his student activism is now simply a means to any material end. Back then his brazenly unscrupulous declaration had shocked the idealistic Dongo who, from what he had only learnt from radio and paper, admired and aligned with the young man's anti-government verve; until he met him in flesh mouthing this profanely disappointing utterance. He had added, that night at his special hangout at Mario Bar, Ekounou, that he was fundamentally an anarchist who had lost fate in change. They had remained friends; but with Dongo maintaining what he termed a 'sane and moral distance' from his anarchist student friend. Until now that he had to need him. This was already the *Che*'s' ninth year in university. An eternal Pol. Science student, his agitated eyes, his ever shining moon head and his Savimbi-like beard – carried over from a dead epoch – were one of the most well known presences in the Faculty of Letters and Humanities. Yes, Ekanga, that's the square man for job! He won't just resist 500.000!

He eventually calls up Ekanga and explains the deal to the young man. Ekanga, as Dongo has truly predicted, finds the whole scheme irresistible and even urges Dongo to consider his role as already played. *Le jeu est bon,* he says into the phone. They slate a rendezvous that day for five at Mario Bar, Ekounou, for the finalization of their deal.

* * * *

The competition is eventually launched and Dongo presides over the jury of eminent dons of Letters drawn from the Arts Faculties of the universities of Yaoundé I, Buea, Dschang and Ngaoundere. To these are sprinkled some established artists and writers. Dongo feels it an immense pride and privilege to preside over a gathering of such eminent personalities – people whom he had in the past often read about in the papers, listen to only on radios and seen only on television. Now here he is, presiding over their sessions, supervising, directing, telling them to be open-minded and fair so that they can come out with representative works that most ideally combined theme and beauty, works whose selection will inspire and express indisputable consensus. Here he is, also reminding them of the importance of the competition, waxing quite patriotic as he spoke, almost declaiming, of how it is a project whose 'spirit is aimed at representing the new national renaissance'.

Two weeks of individual critical work has passed for the jury. The collegiate selection process is now under way. Dongo's first nervous crisis comes in the preliminaries: it becomes decidedly definite that the "O Cameroon" piece has to be eliminated for its archaic language; a kind of 'National Anthem *bis*', the critic besides him mocks, laughing; 'an ersatz copy and a desecrating plagiarism of that august Fonlonian hymn', another don slammed; 'its lack of local poetic feel and colour is lamentably execrable' a writer reproves; and another assessor, a don, dismisses the piece as 'downright sloganeering – very schmaltzy, mediocre and puerile!' This butchering very much offends Dongo. He is fighting real hard to camouflage his rage by pretending, drawing raging worms on his bloc-note, to be taking down the scathing observations. He remembers early on when he had been full of hopes and dreams, how amicable he had been with these men and women of letters. Now he is fighting beyond himself not to call them foes. Now that their critical pens could, on impulse, become butchers' knives. Butchering poems. Butchering millions. And butchering dreams of escaping misery and debts.

He becomes quite ashamed of himself when, through his very ostentatious reading glasses, he looks down at the notebook before him: he has spent that lofty presidency of his scribbling some cryptic pre-nursery script that he himself cannot decipher. Furtively, he crosses those scribbled worms. Dongo brings out a handkerchief, takes off those glasses he had specially bought for his presidency. He holds them low from the left stem and wipes them. He lowers his head and secretly wipes a tear that has welled uncontrollably to his eye. Holding the two stems now with his two hands, he wears them back with brave calm and dignity. He is surprised by the relief and inner peace he now feels. He puts his pen down, closes his notebook and denies himself all forms of writing while the virulent judgment rages on. He now listens to all criticism, caustic or constructive, with unmelting equanimity. He reminds himself definitely that he was just a neutral president of jury. His predicament needs a solution far out of this hostile turf. He concludes.

With that final and irrevocable elimination of the 'O Cameroon' poem and the rest of the jury gone home for the day, Dongo now sits at the end of the long conference table, from where he had presided. He wears a long sunken face, the deep dark face of his uncosmetic feelings. His soul is drained dry of its initial enthusiasm. His mind is drifting far away into a new scheme of including his poem into the winning list. He looks around at the twelve empty spaces of the twelve faces that have been busy exchanging opinions on the works stacked before them. He looks up the wall of the conference hall. The framed effigy of the President of the Republic looks back at him. He tries to convince his mind that even the President of the Republic has herself sometimes cheated. Haven't elections been loudly contested all the times? Hadn't she always placed tribesmen of averred incompetence and corrupt morals in some offices for eternity? Hadn't she lied to the people about certain things? Hadn't she made promises she knows she will never fulfill? He looks up at her Excellency's solemn effigy once more. He turns his face, stands up, tie loose, coat unbuttoned and hands in pocket. He walks around the table thinking. Dongo can cheat for once too...let he who has never cheated in this number one corrupt country throw the first stone...

Mais ils se trompent, je ne baisserai pas le bras! Dongo swore with a sudden anger, whose storm, emboldened by his present solitude, continues to rapidly flaw the less-than-skin-deep mascara of his erstwhile stolidity. He is now fanatically contemplating a kamikaze last-ditch scheme. He has a very extreme way out in gestation. Dongo knows he has a kind of final word. He is the one charged with taking the final results decided by the jury to the minister in charge of the competition.

* * * *

STUDENT ANARCHIST GRABS NATIONAL PATRIOTIC ARTS PRIZE! That is the front page headline splashed this morning on the radical opposition paper, *The Daily Debate*. But since the official declaration of the winner last Saturday, Dongo has been receiving a barrage of calls from all quarters. The minister himself had called, especially when the infuriated members of the jury had stormed his office to disclaim the winning entry. The dons were more discrete, but Dongo's nightmare was coming from the writer members of the jury. Bassey Tenshong, the poet, was already making devastating statements to whosoever cared in the media to question him on the issue. The matter is quickly getting out of hand. The minister has ordered an enquiry.

* * * *

Dongo's phone has become his most nightmarish possession once more. He is thinking of even discarding it. He can't go home, it has becomes a shameful and scary place to go to. His office to him has become a close stop over to Kondengui Prison. His last refuge is now his ever-moving Lada. His last hope is Ekanga Nerius.

Ekanga beeped him last Saturday night, after receiving the trophy and the cheque from the minister's hands at the Hilton Hotel ceremony. During that ceremony, Dongo had distanced himself from Ekanga for obvious reasons. He had called Ekanga back, from a callbox, late in the night after the ceremony and they had fixed a rendezvous at 4pm at Mario Bar-Ekounou.

He is already there and Ekanga is no where around. He grabs his phone angrily from his pocket dials Ekanga's number; remembers he must not call from his own phone. Goes over to the callbox under the parasol outside. Calls. The phone is ringing but is not picked up. Dials again. It rings but is stopped. He dials again and again. The answering machine welcomes him. Instantly, the phone becomes all wet with sweat from the palm of his trembling hand. Ekanga has vamoosed with all of the three million first prize. The dread catches him real. He quakes.

* * * *

—Yes, Manga, it's Dongo calling. I'm calling from a callbox near *Fonction Publique.*

—*Oui*, what's the matter? You sound agitated.

—Please don't ask questions right now. I want you to do me a favour, *camarade*.

—What's that?

—I know you have connections in the Police, the Gendarmerie and just everywhere.

—Yes.

—There's this young man of mine, Ekanga Nerius, who has just burgled my house and made away with three millions.

—Three millions!

—*Je te dis frère, trois millions!* Please do anything you can to get the boy for me.

—Excuse me a minute.

—Yes

—Isn't Ekanga Nerius a name I know?

—Yes, you know him well.

—Let's be serious, Dongo. This guy just won the National Arts Prize a few days ago and the whole thing was all over the press. How could he burgle your house for the exact amount he took home as cash prize? And almost at the same time for that matter!

—Ehm… Dongo wanted to say something but could not find convincing words. And his friend cut him:

—Anyway, he is a popular guy; I will contact my security friends.

Dongo drops the phone abruptly. He doesn't say any goodbye to his friend Manga. Manga's doubts are quite in place and Dongo is kind of caught in his game. His humiliations are reaching no end. Dongo pays the callbox girl, abandons the change with her and runs into his car. He bangs the doors of the Lada close and ignites it with savage rage. He drives with the same fury towards the lake. Other drivers and pedestrians are hooting and cursing as he speeds by with no respect for traffic rules. He gives no damn. He is heading for the deep waters, a pedestrian jokes. He keeps his flight straight on towards his favourite Lakeside drive.

* * * *

Manga has been on a one-week mission up to the Northern provinces on an installation tour with his minister. He arrived in town this morning. On his way home he tells his driver to stop the car in front of the Finance Building by the green Messapresse kiosk.

Dinga calls for the seller to bring *La Gazette* and *Le Débat Quotidien*, the French version of the *Daily Debate*. A girl makes her way through the semi-circular cluster of eager headline and front-page readers, and brings over the requested papers. The two main stories dishearten Manga. Ekanga, caught somewhere near Garoua-Boulai and brought to Yaoundé by the Forces of Law and Order, has made shattering revelations about his dealings with Dongo. As for Dongo, he reads about the Lada that drowned in the Municipal Lake with its owner, a couple of days ago. He crumples all the papers and throws them out of the car window. A hawker picks them up. His driver pulls off without another word.

A Lie Has a Short Life
Eunice Ngongkum

Baamoh left that morning for the road with the lingering feeling that the day was not going to be an ordinary one. The atmosphere in which the students had ended discussions the night before had been particularly tense. They were resolved. The threat of imported troops meant little to them now. Government must do something about their conditions. The memoranda they had written times without number to the powers that be must now bear fruit. There was no going back. Government will either eat its promises or birth them to improve the students' lot. The boy's mind went back to the past week of the strike. The university bosses had betrayed surprising incompetence in handling the crisis. Not because they couldn't but just because they wouldn't. The Prince of the region had stepped in. The students were happy. The *chef de region* would give them satisfaction. He was lord of the place. He was the first and the last. Hadn't he already shown enough good will by ordering the release of the six of the notorious Tenth Police Station? He had. He was open to dialogue. He would do more. Where then had this sudden decision to call in troops from Fedala come from? What had the students done? For all Baamoh knew, the students were warming up for the historic forum with the authorities as the Prince had intimated. Who could have poisoned the man's mind? It could only be the university authorities, the young man reckoned. The Prince was new to the region. These devils might just have taken advantage to give the understanding man a terrible impression about the students. They were capable of this. If last time Gangwe, Tembenn and Efaka were expelled from the university and arraigned before the courts in Vembe, it was thanks to them. They had instigated the previous Prince to drum up ridiculous charges against these student union leaders. Destruction of state property, instigating violence in a peace loving state, enemies of progress, enemies in the house, vectors of division in a country priding itself in twenty years of a unity of its disparate parts…. What all this had to do with a simple student strike could not be understood. Anger welled up in Baamoh. What did these people want? They could have handled matters if they had the mind to. They could. But no, they excelled in sowing division so they could rule the campus with impunity. And now Gangwe, Tembenn and Efaka were wallowing in Dangigi Prison for treason. No wonder the fiends openly rejoiced at the situation.

'Serves them right,' some were heard to say. 'Just how could they expect to act with such impunity here and get away with it, enh? This is an institution built on the rule of law. Destroying property in such great magnitude? Ah no, they even merit the death sentence, come to think of it.' As for the rest of the student body, it was a momentary goodbye to strike action, many of them having been cowed into silence for fear of further reprisals. But hostilities between the students and the authorities of this prestigious establishment were bound to arise anytime. It was simple. On the hills of this distinguished institution, the students looked for justice but saw only wickedness. They cried for understanding but found only a calculated insolence and indifference to their plight. The authorities took delight in deceit. Indeed they were masters in the art. The students had genuine grievances which a perceptive government would have addressed. But not in Vembe or should I say, not in the United Republic of Nahzagha. To tell you the truth, the government with all its big talk was as insensitive to the sufferings of the people as insensitivity could be. More than nine of its eleven million inhabitants lived below the poverty line. But while this majority chose to groan under the weight of structural adjustment programmes, meekly submitting to one indignity after another, the student population of Vembe chose the path of strikes to register its disgust with the system and obtain what they knew were their rights. Having virtually exhausted all avenues of peace, they reckoned this was the only language their authorities understood. And so the strikes returned, and each time in greater intensity like rivers of surging waters.

'What sort of place is this?' Baamoh pondered as he and his friend Willy Fossung took the winding path from his *mini-cité* unto the main road leading into town. 'What sort of people are these? Ha, our authorities. Always succeeding somehow in breaking our resolve. I remember last time. Our full mobilisation. Our determination not to let go until our conditions improved. Broken. Uhm, that rector, that butcher of humanity. Coming to speak to us, and pwang! We all went weak at the knees. Just like that, can you imagine? We all just went weak. I wonder what he has to cast such a spell on us.' The young man shook his head sadly, trying to understand. 'Anyway,' he spoke aloud to no one in particular. 'It will not work. I say this time around, that his magic will just not work.' The voice had risen. Willy turned to him in surprise, wondering whether another student had joined them. There was none. Baamoh stopped talking and looked down. His hands had unconsciously curled up like a boxer's ready to punch his opponent. He chuckled, slowly loosening his tightened fists and letting the hands fall to his sides. He stood quietly for a few minutes, quite oblivious of Willy's presence. Then he picked up his walk again with renewed vigour. The momentary stop seemed to have fuelled his resolve. Willy too stood for a while, bemused, his tongue strangely stuck to the roof of his mouth.

'We are going to stand,' the student union leader pursued, saying the words slowly, deliberately. 'We will do all in our power to stand. Things must change in this place. No wind will move us,' he concluded, walking on, determination in his steps. Willy Fossung followed in perplexed silence.

* * * *

The young man's actions and thoughts could not be said to be the fruit of self-centredness. He had just turned nineteen and was in his last year in the university. In fact, if the strike action were to end now, he would have exactly six months to finish the three outstanding courses required for a BA in History. He had sailed through fairly easily. Most of his teachers had openly commended his application to work. He was so unlike many of the students who peopled Vembe, spending their time in non academic pursuits only to wake up one day to the graduation of classmates and friends. Graduation time brought sudden realisation. They might end up spending more time in the university than they should. Then the man hunt for marks began. It took different routes depending on the individual. There was the avenue of outright cheating known here as *cartouche*, there was the runway of sexually transmissible marks, the bane of young girls. Then there was the more recent and deadly one;

open threats of physical elimination of those lecturers whose strict posture gave the lie to these desperate ones. This was Vembe, the place of morals. This was Univembe the place to be. Baamoh was ready to sacrifice even this last year to ensure a bright future for incoming Univembians. This was a personal crusade, a personal odyssey. Looking at the tall, lanky fair-skinned youth would never suggest the charismatic leader he now was. If he were to be asked, he would truly be unable to say how he had graduated from the shy, soft-spoken fellow of secondary school fame to the tough-talking, no-nonsense student union leader of Univembe repute. In effect, his education in the very religious Lawanda Protestant College prepared him for a life time of moderation; moderation in his outlook on life, ready to cut the middle path whenever and wherever. Even his own home upbringing typically prepared him for the man of peace; the man who would not hurt a fly, who would turn the other cheek for the opponent to slap. His parents were very religious people and raised their children accordingly. Where then was this sudden radicalism from? Something had happened to this young man on the hills of Vembe. Perhaps it was true that those who want peace must prepare for war. Baamoh had slowly come to this conclusion after failed attempts by the student body to press home the demand for their rights. Repeated failure made bold the lad who would stop at nothing to see justice and right prevail here. He was even ready to sacrifice his life for this cause if it came to it. He had sufficiently sounded this way to the enlarged student body the evening before. Their informant from the ranks of the forces of law and order had come to brief them on recent developments in town.

'Military tanks, fire rockets and truckloads of gendarmes are here.' The man sounded worried. 'The Prince of our region has asked for this help from the Prince of the neighbouring Fedala to quell what he calls secessionist riots.'

'Secessionist riots?' the students chorused, surprised. The man nodded slowly. Shock and disbelief were written all over the children. After a moment, several voices rose in anger.

'This is not true.'

'Who is seceding?'

'This is funny, indeed.'

'Who is talking of secession?'

'These people are jokers.'

'No, I think they must be downright crazy, you know.'

'Massa, you fit imagine dis guys them?' One dark skinned boy asked, turning to his neighbour on the left, his eyes bloodshot. 'Imagine some *nyiè* people oh. Secession, *oui*,' he laughed with difficulty.

The informant raised his hand timidly to call for calm. It was evident that he had not finished. The angry reactions gave the impression that he was the one who had actually called them secessionists. He was clearly uneasy. Baamoh sat very quietly on the high table, flanked by two of his close allies. His arms, folded across his chest, rested on the table. He watched his fellow schoolmates keenly. An unusual smile played at the corners of his lips and his eyes twinkled in some kind of amusement. The informant was speaking.

'Yes, he calls them secessionist riots. But that is not why I am here, children. My reason for coming here this night is to give you warning.' He was grave. 'Please, I beg you; do not for any reason venture out tomorrow. Do not go to the main road. I repeat, none of you should be found anywhere near the road leading into Vembe tomorrow. Tell your friends who are not here. The road tomorrow is forbidden to all students.'

'Why?' the students queried. 'Why shouldn't we go to the road? What is on the road?'

'Well, my dear students,' the man answered. 'Orders have been given to these foreign troops to shoot down any moving thing. And you know these gendarmes are not from here.' He stopped, to let what he was saying sink in.

'These forces have already taken up position in strategic areas here in town.' The man paused again, swallowed hard before continuing. 'You see, the authorities are not taking it kindly that you held the Tenth Police Station hostage for close to three hours and forced the commissioner to release your detained schoolmates. Your victory irritates the Prince like smoke in one's eyes. Someone told him releasing those students was a sign of weakness. He wants to prove that he can sufficiently handle the situation. This then is the way he intends to do it, using tougher measures despite advice to the contrary from his immediate collaborators. So I say again dear students, no road for any of you tomorrow if you value your life. Don't say I did not warn you.' Sweat glistened on the man's forehead by the time he finished speaking. He removed a yellow handkerchief from his pocket, wiped his face and slowly made his way to the door. The students were quiet, watching. The man reached the door, opened it and walked out. Baamoh sat glued to his chair staring ahead of him. No one spoke for what seemed like a decade. Then he jumped to his feet. All eyes turned to him. He straightened the red T-shirt he was wearing, looked around briefly and then cleared his throat.

'We will go to the road.' The words seemed to be discharged from an overloaded Dane gun. The silence was eerie. The voice rose. 'Comrades, I say, we have no choice but the road.' He slowly looked around, daring anyone to contradict him. 'We must go to the road, gendarmes or no gendarmes. They cannot frighten us. If they will not listen to us, there is no other option but the road.' Baamoh paused again. 'Come to think of it my friends, is it war? I ask you, are we fighting a war with them? Calling in truckloads of gendarmes, hah? They are not serious. Who are they coming to fight, huengh? Who are these people really coming to fight? Defenceless, armless students, is that right? We are nothing but dead dogs. And they come to fight us. Is this their idea of negotiation? Is this what the Prince means by asking us to the negotiating table? Talk of dialogue, enh? This is his idea of dialogue, I dare say. Tanks, armoury and troops.' He looked down, shaking his head slowly. 'No comrades, no. We must continue to the end.'

These last words were spoken almost in a whisper. Then the young man looked up suddenly. Fire was in his eyes. The burning members ranged the length and breadth of the room challenging, pleading, coaxing, and daring the more than two hundred pairs of eyes looking up. The intense look hurled defiance at the threats. It summoned fiery resistance from those present. The gaze was to be long remembered for days to come.

* * * *

Vembe, the capital of the Western Region of the United Republic of Nahzagha, was linked to Fedala, the capital of the South Eastern Region, by some fifty kilometres of tarred road. It was a growing town whose outlook betrayed the character of the people of these parts and the quality of their relations with the rest of the country. The people here were known for their outspokenness. They were so vocal that the other Nahzaghans looked up to them when it came to matters of justice and right. The western regionists alone gave sleepless nights to the rulers. They were known to dissect and condemn any decision taken by the authorities that was clearly unfavourable to the majority. What Nahzaghans grumbled about in the dark, the westerners brought to the light. The western region was to Nahzagha what the head is to the body. One illustration will suffice. In the not too distant past, civil servants' salaries were slashed by more than three quarters, thanks to the economic crisis. One north easterner left one morning for his bank in downtown Andale, capital of the country, to collect his monthly pay cheque. He could not believe what the cashier handed to him. He turned to the people standing there, holding out the few notes for all to see. Getting no response from the bystanders, he exclaimed in desperation.

'*Ce n'est pas possible ça. Mon Dieu, est ce que les Regionists de l'Ouest ont vu ça? Merde! Et qu'est ce qu'ils font, hein?*' The man was clearly overwhelmed. Poor man. Salvation in this particular matter was never to come from the West. The economic crisis had imprisoned the spirit of the whole nation, choking the life out of the people. There was no will left to fight. Only the will to survive. And survival was not bedfellows with outspokenness even with the vocal westerner. A culture of silent submission to the arrogance of high office overtook the country. The people, like sheep led to the slaughter, were mute recipients of the endless instruments of pain and official highhandedness. But not the students of Vembe, offspring of the nation's conscience. They refused to learn passivity. Here at Univembe, the fire to fight, to challenge evil was alive. After all, this citadel of learning was the fruit of united and determined struggle. The West had sacrificed even life to have it here. The jewel, lying at the foot of the majestic Vembe heights, spoke the region's language, which the population was trying to ignore but which the students relished: 'Never give in to what is wrong. Always stand up for what is right.'

* * * *

Baamoh reflected more and more about this state of affairs as the strike action entered a decisive state. The courses he was taking in Nazagha history were opening his intellectual antennae to exciting historical discoveries about Vembe, the students, and the peculiar place of the western region in the context of the nation. Why did a normal student strike that went almost unnoticed in the other state universities assume diabolic proportions when it came to Vembe? Why did the Prince now view it as secession? Did the Prince who was not from these parts have a hidden agenda? Was there a secret ploy to destroy what the West stood for? Were some Westerners themselves greedy for personal gain responsible for the present plight of the region? After all as history revealed, the political naivety of the Westerner was responsible for the marginalisation the region today suffered. As things unfolded daily, pieces of the jigsaw puzzle fell into place. The boy began to understand the peculiar status of the westerner in the country. The fact that the military headquarters of the region was in the neighbouring South East took on new meaning. A neighbouring people of a different tongue. Who knew only one language when it came to his people. The language of suppression, the language of violence. *'Ces gens ci, ces Regionists de l'Ouest, ils se croient où ici? Ils vont nous sentir!'*

Baamoh shuddered in recollection. He had once taken a trip to the neighbouring Fedala to visit a cousin living there. He vividly recalled the linguistic battle he had fought with a police officer. Baamoh had insisted on speaking the language of the West which the man did not want to understand even though it was beautifully enshrined in the constitution of the republic. The man had demanded that the young man express himself in the language of the South East. Baamoh had resisted. Were it not for the timely intervention of his host, things would have taken a turn for the worse. The contorted face of the enraged officer emerged from a buried past to haunt him now with their presence in Vembe. It also paradoxically fired the lad with resolve.

* * * *

The student union executive bureau was holding a crucial meeting to finalise the programme for the next day. Just then, one of the publicity secretaries burst into the room in excitement: 'Massa they de talk for town say you are part of a movement fighting for the secession of the western region from the rest of the country. The gendarmes are coming here with this knowledge oh. They are already there. I saw them.' He sat down on a chair near the door. The discussions momentarily ceased. After a while Kujum, the financial secretary, spoke.

'Bros, I think we should lie low for some time. If nothing

substantial happens, then we take to the road again. What do you think?' He looked to the others for approval. The technical adviser and the secretary general nodded in agreement. The other five members were not quite decided. Baamoh looked at them for some time. All the others seemed to be waiting for him to conclude the matter. After a while he stood up.

'My friends,' he began. 'My able comrades, we must not stop now. We have to go on. This is the time to press on to the end. See, we have scored some victories because we were steadfast. Our school mates were released. The two thousand francs for examination material abolished. Let us press on for the remaining demands; the school fees, food, water on campus and good hostels. Our leaders understand only one language, Persistence. If we give up now,' he paused. 'I say if we give up now, our situation will become worse than before. Remember, wickedness and violence are like food and drink to our leaders. This will be our portion if we were to stop now.' His demeanour was now stern. 'Now, who wants to quit? Please stand up and walk out through that door now. If we must die to bring sanity to our institution, then I am ready. Who will go with me?' He held out his right hand. All the executive members got up silently and placed their hands in his. None walked out. The meeting rose for the night.

Baamoh was inwardly elated. This was unheard of. The union leaders in total agreement? This was news. The authorities had succeeded in time past to brew division among them and it ate into the entire student body. The tribal factor held sway. The indigenous students of Vembe were told that those from the peripheries were jealous of the development of their town, of their university. The strike action was their pretext to destroy Vembe and take over control. The authorities had succeeded at the time. But today it was different. The entire student body, beginning with the executive, understood that there was no tribe when it came to suffering. Indeed, suffering was pronounced the same in all the languages of the region. A few in Vembe might be finding life easy but not the majority. These suffered the same deprivations, the same frustrations like the rest from the Western Region. The lie of the tribe had failed. A lie has a short life. The boy smiled in the dark. The students were now all mobilised like one man around the cause. He savoured this newfound unity with gusto as he walked home from the meeting. The pleasure of it seemed to burst out of him.

A Lie Has a Short Life

* * * *

The young man heaved himself out of bed. His body felt like the property of someone else. What was the matter now? He sighed as his feet touched the cold floor. He sat on the bed for a while trying to recollect himself. A swarm of birds was having a heated debate in his head. He raised his hands to support it while making a big effort to understand what the matter really was. To add insult to injury, he felt as if his flesh and muscles were being eaten away. Could it be the onset of malaria? Could it be exhaustion? Curling up in bed and going back to sleep seemed the only logical thing to do. But hell, no. The planned meeting at the road this morning. My God, I can't afford sleep today. We must march up to the Prince as we decided. We must tender our memo to him. We will not budge until he gives us a favourable answer. We want to negotiate. One does not reject dialogue. He called us to talk things over with him. We will go. We will ignore the military presence in our town. We will act responsibly. We have often been accused of irresponsibility. No, we will go marching peacefully. My flesh and muscles cannot fail me now. Sleep, see you later. He stood up with deliberateness and shuffled into the bathroom to clean up.

He came back in, took down his jeans trousers and red T-shirt from the nail on the wall and got into them. He sat down on the bed, sent his right hand under and pulled out his tennis shoes. He slipped the first one on, then the other. He stood up and walked to the left side of the room where the gas stove stood. He lighted it and then put the pot of left-over rice on it to get warm. He moved over to the table. The memo was lying there. Baamoh picked it up and as he looked at it, he told himself that this was not the time to chicken out. We must press on to the end, he reminded himself. He imagined what would happen if they did not follow through. He shuddered with fear at the uplifted hand of the authorities. He did not want to go the way of past student leaders. He wanted to plant a name on the sands of time. He would enjoy the moment of victory when future Univembians would hail him as the man who fought for better conditions in the institution. His name would go down in the annals of the university. The moment of glory would be exhilarating… His cell phone rang. It was his mother.

'Hello, Mama,' Baamoh responded from his end.

'How are you my boy, how are things?'

'Fine.'

'So what is happening? I hear you people are on strike again?' He answered in the affirmative. Mama continued. 'I hope you are not involved in it my son. I hope you are not.' There was no response.

'Bam, Bam are you getting me?'

'I am getting you Mama,' he answered with difficulty. 'We are just trying to state our point, Ma. You see, I cannot stay away because I am a part of the institution. We must all sacrifice if things…' His mother did not allow him to finish.

'Yes sonny, I agree with you. You must state your point. You must sacrifice. I am okay with that. But my child, you know our leaders. How they can react. So please be careful. Do not be involved in any form of violence. You can make your point without recourse to violence.' Baamoh heard a car honk. Mama was speaking.

'That is your father. I am off to work. Talk to you later, okay?'

'Okay, Mama. Please greet Nelly, Inah and Dad for me.' She hung up.

The pot on the stove was now burning. Baamoh quickly switched off the fire and went for a plate. There was no clean one in the cupboard. He went to the sink, rapidly rinsed one and dished himself some food. He pulled out the chair and sat down.

'Just like Mama. She will die if she gets to know that I am the one leading the strike this time.' His heart sank. 'Does she know?' he shook his head slowly. 'Maybe. But who would have told her?' he shrugged his shoulders, shaking his head in denial at the same time. 'No. I don't think she knows. She would have asked me directly. Maybe she just has some presentiment. I know her.' He chuckled to himself. 'Mama, I am waiting to see her face when I tell her that I was the leader of the strike. She will collapse. But wait a minute. Has she heard anything about the troop deployment? Perhaps. I think I should call her back and find out more. I still have some credit.' He picked up the phone and was about to dial the number when Willy Fossung, the secretary general of the student union, knocked and entered.

'Old boy, what's up? It is almost nine, my man. The students are already in their numbers waiting for you. Let's go, massa.'

Baamoh stood up from the table, picked up the plate of rice, placed it on the gas stove and walked out with his friend.

* * * *

The main road was a sea of students when the two boys arrived. The whole university had emptied itself unto the road. The sun was shining brightly and there was no trace of rain bearing clouds on this beautiful September morning. No vehicles were in sight. The students had erected a human barrier across the breadth of the narrow road impeding the flow of traffic. Curious onlookers lined both sides of the road, wondering what the students were up to this time around. The atmosphere was charged. One could almost feel and touch the tension in the air. The restiveness was fuelled by the songs of the students.

> Our victory is on the way
> Our victory is on the way
> Our victory is on the way even now
> Our victory is on the way even now.

> There will be freedom in this place
> Freedom and sanity in this place
> There will be freedom in this place even now
> Freedom and sanity in this place even now.

* * * *

As soon as Baamoh appeared, shouts and ululations rent the sky. The students took up his welcome chant, 'President, president, president, president.' Tree branches miraculously emerged as if the equatorial forest at Jeesen had elected today to register its objection to wanton pillage. A makeshift stand of drums and broken chairs held together by old twines was brought to the front and Baamoh hoisted unto it to address the assembly. He raised his hand and immediately, there was silence. One could hear a pin drop. The lad surveyed the sea of heads, cleared his throat and then began.

'Fellow comrades,' the voice rang out, loud and clear. 'I welcome you all. I am glad you are all here in your numbers this morning. It is proof of our commitment to the cause of Univembe. We have been called all sorts of names; secessionists, vandals, ingrates, you name them.' He paused. 'But we are people of peace. We will therefore march up peacefully to the Prince of our Region and tender in our memo. We will stay put until he satisfies us, isn't it?'

'Yeeeeees, President,' the crowd roared. Meanwhile, just to

Baamoh's right, a stupefying horde of military tanks and men in combat ready attire was advancing slowly towards the student body. Baamoh turned to look at them, fascinated. When it stopped about three hundred metres away from them, the boy turned again to his schoolmates.

'This is ridiculous,' he stopped to let the effect of what he had observed sink in. 'You see my comrades,' he went on. 'You see our rulers? This,' he pointed to the combat ready troops, 'is their response to our peaceful demands for better living conditions. This is dialogue brothers, sisters.' Baamoh laughed in derision. 'This is dialogue. But we shall not be intimidated. We must not give up. We must stand for what we know is our due even to the last ounce of blood in our veins.' The grim determination had returned to the voice and he was almost shouting. 'We are not fighting a war. We are not criminals. We only want to have what is our right. Now as I said before, we are here to go up to our Prince. We will dialogue with him. Up comrades, up we go.' He intoned the song, 'there will be victory in this place....'

The students did not allow their coordinator to finish. They rose as one man with a mighty shout bringing the tremors to the foundations of Vembe. Something had gone terribly wrong. Instead of starting out for the Prince's office, the advancing students turned on the military forces with rage, chanting and waving their palm branches. Some booed while others jeered the men. Someone had lifted Baamoh from the makeshift rostrum and thrust him to the front. He found himself at the head of the marching throng. A palm frond was pressed into his hand. The military men began retreating as the students advanced on them. You could see uneasiness and uncertainty in their mien. It was just a matter of seconds and the students would overwhelm the forces. Then it happened. Gunshots tore the morning sky and then there was total confusion.

* * * *

Some of the onlookers said that when he was shot, Baamoh Itiabi kept marching forward with that same determination with which he had addressed his fellow students. He apparently was not aware of what had happened to him until he fell on the gendarme officer who shot him, his blood and intestines spilling out. The man merely pushed the body away and moved on.

109

THE LOST ART
Job Fongho Tende

Yaoundé, 2150 A.D.…

It is also a mark of beauty to judge not from mere appearance; it is a trait of aesthetics to understand an individual not only from the things he seems to say or do, but also as a being with needs and whose mind feeds on historical data. This data, in times of need, connects the individual to historical realities, thus providing a kind of shoulder on which the individual may rest…

The city was in its customary air of deceptive tranquility, with birds soaring the blue firmament in whose clouds the city's skyscrapers hid their heads. It was not common to find the sun during this period of the year, the rainy season, but on that day the sun was unusually determined to break out of anonymity. The heavenly bodies fought to shine over the fast changing city of Yaoundé. But if the moon and stars had let themselves be cheated of their glory by the obscuring brightness of the hundreds of street bulbs in the place, the sun was in no way showing signs of negotiating its own glory.

The sound from vehicular traffic, moving along the streets, converged into a hostile crude rhythm irreconcilable to the city's artificial look. All these put together made it hard for the mind to conceive the existence of natural and seemingly rural site like Mvolye, planted almost in central Yaoundé.

In the very heart of this metropolis, Mvolye seemed so faraway — not in perspectives of space. With its colossal cathedral, mainly of wood, its grassy vegetation and stony terrain, it appeared as odd as would a piece of hot desert amidst an archipelago.

Meko lived in one of the city's peripheral neighbourhoods, Mvan to be precise. But his life found meaning in the milieu of the natural and rural air characteristic of the Mvolye hill. The Mvan suburb was far less sophisticated than central sectors like Mvog-Ada, Njongolo,

Etoudi, and Ngoa et Kele. In fact only the Mvolye hillside could be compared to Mvan, clue that it was not just the ruralness of the hillside alone that drew his heart there. There was definitely something else that bound the old Meko's heart to Mvolye, something which defying words, impelled the ripe man to cover on bicycle the 3km between Mvan and Mvolye.

At 67, Meko had lived long enough to witness the strife between state and church, notably the Catholic Church. He had seen whole properties formerly owned by the church taken over by State: schools and other learning centres, monasteries, hospitals, supermarkets, cathedrals, orphanages etc. Also he was not unaware that according to the recent state reforms it was a strict prohibition for anyone in the country, who cherished their lives and liberty, to identify with anything religious, especially the Catholic body. And for such associations, many had had to pay the supreme price, their lives.

If asked, Meko was quite at a loss explaining why the state had suddenly adopted such drastic measures against the church. Rumours circulated, and according to the most popular the state, for reasons still buried in shadows, had met with stiff opposition from the enlightened clergies. The men of God suspected the state of anti-christic manoeuvres; they read in the new politico-religious reforms the states intention to establish the abominable sacrilege predicted in the holy scriptures: *When you see the abomination that causes desolation standing where it does not belong — let the reader understand- then let those who are in Judea flee to the mountains. (Mk 13:14)* How dare the State attempt to usurp the place of God in the hearts of men…? There is but one Lord… And He that sits on high and reigns, it's to Him that belong the hearts of all men.

Twenty-five years now, if anything, the gulf between state and Church had only grown wider and wider. The church was officially unofficialised, and anyone who in any way identified themselves with her was by the very reason of such association declared state enemy. Needless to say that a bunch of Christians made quit of their church practices, neither observing their spiritual duties in public or in private. How convincing and convicting the State proved to be! However few they were, those who from the bottom of their hearts had sworn an eternal allegiance to the God of heaven, continued with the church in the shadows of the city's blind alleys, and this at their peril.

Meko was descendant of a long lineage of Bantu craftsmen. His ancestors were the great forest men of old reputed for their dexterity in the shaping of wood, clay and stone into different forms and instruments: masks, balafons, canoes, gongs and flutes. In those days the forest used to resonate with the beats of their untamed savage splendour born of their craft; not mastered by foreign winds. That was many centuries ago. Yaoundé was now a modern city, a very modern city irreconcilable to that part of itself.

That forest home of his ancestors was no more; it had inevitability given way to this place of concrete and streets. Things which were the very expression of his people's existence had been more or less relegated to the benefit of exotic ways. Even Meko, despite his many years, lacked that stirring enthusiasm for such things like the masks, balafons and tam-tams. If he had failed in his responsibility to emulate his ancestors in their ever fresh passion after the outward expression of their culture, the dead had not failed to communicate down to him those very gins to which he owed his prowess in the noble art of sculpture.

That Meko was an accomplished sculptor was the least that could be said of the old man. It was his expertise in this craft, among other issues, that had made his destiny cross with the Roman Catholic faith. An accomplished sculptor, Meko carved stone, wood, marble, and clay into religious statues that occupied a place of honour in the cathedrals and other places of worship belonging to the fidels, now dispersed by terror and error.

If ever there was a man the Governor suspected of criminally collaborating in secret with the church, that man was no other but Meko. He alone continued, in spite of general fear around the business, to carve statuettes of the virgin and celestial beings. But if the Governor bore such suspicions he had no weighty proof to oblige the sculptor to betray the faithfuls. When it came to such things, Meko was no child. Like an experienced artist he knew how to give an artistic look, a commercial look to his works, which were used for religious ends all the same.

'Meko I know you're hiding something from me.'

'Your Excellency, everyone has got secrets you know. Only fools write their mind on the sky for just anyone to see.'

'Meko don't play that game with me. We definitely understand each other. Don't we?'

'Excellency I'm an old man, and a very old man for that matter. If

I should continue to play at this age, what then marks the difference between me now and 50, 40, 30, or 15 years ago?' with rephrase Meko successfully communicated his innuendo.

'Enough with that!' the infuriated Governor snapped.

'Now tell me,' in a tone of menace, disappointed coyness. 'For whom do you sculpt these statuettes?' Pointing at the relics with obvious contempt which Meko does not fail to understand.

'Sir, if it would do you any good, know therefore that I do my work for those with a fine inner appreciation for the magic of arts; for those smart enough to read in this noble profession and its proceeds, profound intellectual…'

'Spare me that scrap!' the furious Governor hushed Meko, who as it were, was carried in a paroxysm of passion, expounding on the virtues of his profession.

'Hmm hmmm, it's like you don't understand that Muggings here listening to you play him can make your old life very miserable scheming against state integrity, oo-ld ma-n.' Fuming with discontentment, the exasperated Governor made the atmosphere tense.

'Is it an offence today in Yaoundé to be a man of arts? Is it wrong done unto the state contributing to the yearly influx of tourists when nowadays tourism appears to be the state's most promising industry?' Meko's intervention made no sense, and he knew it little pleased the man doing the interrogatives.

'You think you are smart. Don't you?' the Governor said, a rueful smile betraying his stifled resentment.

'For the very last time Meko, are you a Roman Catholic?'

Now, the old man, who was busy clothing a statuette of the famous virgin in soft sky-blue, straightened up for the first time to face the man in front of him.

'Are you threatening me, old man that I am, Excellency?'

'No.'

Silence pervades.

'Then know therefore that I am not a Roman Catholic though my travail limits not its efficacy to the secular plain. The old Meko is of no such religious affiliation and the arts thereof.'

'One clear answer at last!' exclaimed the administrator in triumph. 'Meko,' he continued almost without any emotional restraints, 'I hope you know the meaning of the word "blas-phe-my".' He climbed into his military jeep and drove off accompanied by two bodyguards, whom Meko recognised as members of one of the persecuted churches.

The Governor of the Central province, more than any other member of government, had made a personal responsibility to rid the land of its Christian inhabitants. His torture centre was equipped with the most recent pain producing technologies. Many had had their lives virtually squeezed out of their bodies in this centre. For some who entered the camp and came out alive, their Christian convictions never made it out with them. Thanks to his numerous encounters with the Christian breed the Governor understood quite well the people's mentality.

Blasphemy, he knew the Christian community would not tolerate; he had come across a good number of those who once had blasphemed, were filled with such remorse and self spite that they did terrible things even suicide and betrayal of their own Christian brothers. The crafty Governor counted much upon this that he tried to play on Meko's psychology.

Meko watched as the military vehicle rode down the stony descent of the remote Mvolye hill, until it disappeared behind the shades of grass and trees. Then he returned to his brush, colours and statuettes whistling a melody as he gave colour to a piece. Beside him Ngemba, his young apprentice, knelt chiselling a saintly figure out of red wood.

As a young boy Meko had a strong appeal for the stories about the forest people which his father had satisfied his curiosity with. A good narrator, his late father was able to hold him spell bound as he made legends come back to life by the sole strength of his able narration. His late father used to use the chronicles of their ancestors to educate and entertain the small boy that he was. So Meko, through these stories and the enforcement of more practical training, came to understand how his ancestors worked clay, stone, wood and metals to produce items which seemed to have fallen from some benevolent stars.

If today, in his intercourse with the Governor, Meko had pronounced himself and his arts laic, he did not consider it an issue of the relevance of a blasphemy, even though the Governor did. To Meko this was only a blind association with foundations resting in mere illusions.

Though his art fetched his bread and also gave response to a multitude of hungry souls seeking spiritual gratification, it was not the crux of his profession and for that reason he little cared if the Governor or anybody else misunderstood his declarations.

To Meko, sculpture was also that organic fibre that linked him back to his ancestry. It was the invisible stream that washed their better psycho-physical attributes into his more recent and naïve existence. Via sculpture, Meko entered a new universe; one in which his deceased father and the uncountable rows of legendary forest people found an inlet back into the world of the living.

If old Meko was vested with a religion of any kind, that religion found form in his art. Sitting in his private workshop moulding a saintly portrait out of clay, his soft old wrinkled palms would massage and caress the squidgy mould with appeasing tenderness. At the zenith of his ritual, carried away by unconscious movements of fingers and hands repeated over years and centuries, Meko would be teleported to a realm of the immortal forest folks wherein he would fellowship with them by the intermediary of the soul-relieving art. The claim to difference, in his modern office, lay neither in the copied ritualistic movements of fingers and hands nor in the same spirit-liberating effects, but in the material produce of the enterprise. Such was the religion Meko's soul clung to with steadfastness. How then could the blinkered ever understand him?

'...but brother, why did you yield to the enemy even at this hour when the saviour's church suffers a great tribulation? Why could you not stand your grounds? Why did you cede to blasphemy against this holy body of Christ here gathered?' the holy Reverend spoke strongly and yet in a low tone, presumably giving respect to Meko, who was evidently riper in years.

Although a weird wind now threatened the atmosphere, rarely were nights ever star-lit like the one that saw the persecuted gathered. It was during an occasion of the sacrament of the Lord's body. And like Christ's disciples of old were gathered, chased from exposure by the violent world, and kept together by common faith in God, so were the fidels. They had formed a circular assembly in whose centre Meko stood, facing clerical prosecution.

'If our dear brother Meko would now confess his blasphemous utterances and recant thereof, this holy body will admit him to its righteous bosom like one of its own.'

They had judged him already.

For only the blasphemy against the Holy Ghost shall have no allowance unto pardon but that against the Father, the Son and his body share the benefits of divine pardon.'

Light… Greyness… Darkness!

Meko raised his head, the grey patches of his unkempt hair faintly revealed by the departing moon light, and with a slow glance studied his surrounding and noticed the effects of their Reverend's speech on the rest of the people's impressions of his person.

'My beloved Reverend, dear brethren,' he began with what was supposed to be his defence, 'if today I should stand before you and the Spirit of the Lord to recant a view I do not hold, do I make my faith any better than that of those who have no faith? Or brothers…' 'Hold it there Meko!' Before he could explain himself the Reverend broke in like thunder. 'Why do you allow the fouler to harden your fine soul to this point? Though we all may still love you dearly our greater love for the faith impels us to do justice to the Lord of the Church. We, by that greater love declare you no longer one of us. Until you purge your erstwhile holy soul of its actual diabolic intoxications, you remain excommunicated from the fellowship of the faithful.' Meko bit his lower lip in obvious pain and disappointment.

Darkness. Lightning. Hurricane.

'Consequently,' the man of God went on, 'the faithful here and elsewhere shall have nothing to do with you and the works of your hands. That art of yours, blessed of God, which has been a deep source of consolation and exhortation to his children persecuted everywhere, has now been desecrated by your present betrayal.'

It was under a grumbling dark sky that Meko left the Mvolye gathering on his bicycle. Some minutes before he could reach the security of his home, the skies broke open and the rain that had been menacing that night of March, drenched him copiously.

A log of wood cracked and glowed red in the open hearth. Meko sat alone warming himself there. His mind could scarcely abandon the gathering which he had left behind on the Mvolye hill.

'Brother so you do admit, by your adamant refusal to recount your blasphemous positions against this body, that you are now of the same crop with the state in its anti-christic designs?'

'I am not against Christ! I have never declared myself as not belonging to his body. And for that reason I feel no liberty inside recanting a view I don't and will never hold…'

The interview returned to him over and over again with almost the same or sharper pains as the glowing hearth reinforced his corporal heat.

His house was more or less a museum. It contained a variety of carved works ranging from the local wood works of the natives to the sophisticated marble designs of occidental Christianity. While the former consisted of some of his father's works and marked the epoch of his father's existence, the latter identified the period later in his own life when he had given in to the influence of the more western trends in sculpting.

In one of his inner chambers, the one which was his very private workshop, was a beautiful clay portrait of himself. For beauty and resistance, it was lightly coated with a chocolate brown marble. It was in everyway his very replica; his wildly grown hair, his broad nose, tiny eyes and generous lower lip were transplanted onto the carved figure. The figure leant itself on a tree trunk made of clay. The work, but for the absence of its arms which were yet to be fitted in, would have been a complete success. This was no doubt the work through which the artist had made a self dedication. During these tumultuous times when he suffered loneliness, the work transcended the realm of mere artistic beauty; it had become his only family and companion.

At this very ripe age, at 68, Meko was expected to be surrounded by a family of his own: a wife, children and grandchildren. Why not! A dreamer, Meko as a young man habitually probed into the future to get a foretaste of himself as father of a populous family, the pride of the old. In such moments he would picture an old him covered with the grey of age and surrounded by the fruits of his loins. Alas, life had not treated him according to his cherished visions, and his aspirations had never reached fulfilment.

If he had lived long enough to bury his father and mother, his own son had not lived that long to respond to this human tradition. Wife and son had been treacherously snatched from life in a calamitous wreck in the high seas of Limbe during a cultural festival; a festival they had attended with the purpose of auctioning the highly acclaimed works of their father and husband.

Darkness! Darkness! Darkness!

Their graves were built in the recesses of his large compound, and whenever he was, by a situation or need, obliged to pass by them, for he intentionally avoided their sight, he raised his head skywards in evasion.

The Lost Art

Cynthia R. Meko 2092-2140
If only the dead understood the grief they leave behind once
departed, you Cynthia my beloved would have seen my tears daily
flowing and whisper back something to me.
I miss you and will forever do, Love.

George Meko Jr 2120-2140
How too quick this unwelcome sojourner came to you my only
child … O, what grief pervades a day whose sun sets at noon! Here
you lay, life from my life; my ray of hope; the face there was to stand
for my people, stolen away into the other world before your
progenitor. Bye-bye my son!

But these days he found himself kneeling and weeping at the
sepulchre of his long gone family whose absence had, for the past
years, been filled by the fellowship of the faithful. In the faithful he
had found a new family and a new reason to go on with the
laborious responsibility of living. He had found in them a people he
could talk and relate to. A people he could call brother, sister and by
that have a vicarious taste of a filial life and one that his parents had
failed to grant him; a people whose Reverend leader was to him the
father figure long vanished in dust.

'Father… Father… Father' he would whisper faintly, marching
among the other faithful towards the Reverend dispensing the
sacrament of the Lord's body. Kneeling to receive the brittle halves
of the sanctified meal, and feeling its tasteless particles dissolving on
the moisture of his anticipating tongue, Meko would find himself
mentally reeled into reunions with his precursors.

But all these: the sacramental meal and the sweet fellowship of the
faithful, like his own family, had each borrowed an outlet away from
his life leaving him utterly broken. His tears, dropping on the
tombstones of his loved ones made thread-like rivers through their
dust.

By the signs of age Meko understood his end was near and
whatever he still owed the living he had to settle it immediately. If he
had not left behind a descendant it was not his fault. But his fault it
would have been, even heaven knew it, if his apprentice was not
made the heir of his art; the guardian of this skill which spoke deeper
things than just the transformation of raw materials into admirable
forms. So he looked forward to the day when, like his father had

done with him, he would seat the young Ngemba as custodian of his art. Opening before him its sacred origins, its essence and mystery of which he was its living centre. An art which though mysterious in its soul appeasing effects, magical in its widening of the intellect, in no wise converged with mysticism.

' Meko, *tu est convoqué au bureau du gouverneur ce soir à seize heures. Faut pas manquer,*' Ngemba informed Meko one morning. But before Meko could say a thing, the young apprentice had vanished with the wind, leaving behind him the written convocation from the Governor's office, which Meko held in his trembling hands. His mind wondering vainly about what awaited him at the place of rendezvous outlined in the letter.

Later in the evening, before he left for the Governor's, he fearfully noticed the absence of the statue dedicated to himself. Someone had taken advantage of this hour when his soul travelled into darkest night, to plunder him of his sole consolation. An ominous shiver rushed through his old frame and 'Papa God... Papa, mama, Papa God!' A cry of distress came forth unconsciously, as in his fear he evoked the names of those he venerated above himself. He could foresee the infernal web stretched against his life.

Firestorm. Fire masquerades. A star explodes.

'Meko... Meko...' the Governor addressed him with the briskness of an overconfidence assailer. 'Let us not make long a short talk. Are you a Roman Catholic? Where therefore is their hideout?' Meko only offered an impassive glance which at length irritated the senior officer.

'I charge you by the powers conferred to me... speak!' The vexed Governor snapped precipitating his hour of triumph.

'Sir, I don't understand... don't know what you talking about.'

Why do you ruin my life with this bloody inquiry of yours... to hell with you and your evil investigations!

'Since you claim to be a smart old man,' the Governor said 'I shall call a witness whose testimony shall be valid enough to cost those miserable hands of yours just as its expressed in one of your accursed masterpieces.' The old man trembled, not so much for the witness or his testimony or the suggested punishment, but at the allusion made to his replica, the work of his consecration.

'So now, honourable men of your stature go violating an old man's privacy...' Meko burst out without volition against the Governor, who paid little or no attention to the accusation made explicit in

Meko's address.

The office door creaked open, then marched in Ngemba. With his thin needle-like face, Meko sensed that he was out for a purpose hardly orthodox in nature, compelled by unlawful influences.

'Ngemba my boy, is it you that has been elected to speak against me? What have this people promised you child that you come out zealously to accuse me, your father and teacher?' Meko spoke, warm tears rushing down his wrinkled face. Not tears of fear. But tears of the feeling of having been betrayed. Betrayed by his supposed heir, a young man he recruited for free, a boy he had resolved to leave behind as custodian of his noble art. Treacherous existence!

'Do not menace the youth anymore old man,' the Governor intervened in a rather triumphant tone. 'Youngman, say what you must say now!'

'M-e-k-o' he stammered, struggling to choose his words. It was not easy to be that creative. 'Young man talk, do not be afraid.' The Governor urged him. Then Ngemba gradually found stability in the fiendish craft of betrayal.

'… by making a statue of marble, Meko wants to make himself a god; he intends to be a figure of religious influence. This is in defiance not only to Catholic norms but also against state ideologies. He is not only a Catholic, he is worst than all the other Catholics put together…' Then he added a touch which, though was not part of his rehearsal, pleased the sadist construct of the Governor's soul: 'Rid the earth of such gangrene, O Governor.'

His mission finished, Ngemba spirited himself out of the office of military furniture, dreading any eye contact with Meko.

'Meko did you follow the weighty accusations made against you by your closest man?' The Governor asked with criminal excitement. But Meko's mind was too far to hear him, let alone replying. The Governor's metallic voice reached him as the crow of a black hawk one occasionally hears in a difficult sleep.

'Guards take him over to the amputation chambers!' With immediacy the aged fellow was carried away. Before the execution of his punishment, a document was read to him stating his crime and punishment. Like light iron filings after a magnet, the baseless allegations caught up with his elusive life. With all its deficit in judiciary aesthetics the prosecution fatally fell against Meko.

Without any visible, resistance his hands were fitted into the sleeves of the famous amputator whose blades soon betrayed the frailty of flesh and bone. And as prescribed by the law, he was soon rushed for medical care to prevent death by bleeding and pain. 'It is all a funny game,' the medical personnel thought aloud. 'What's the point in these new reforms!' While Meko lay lamenting over his condition, Ngemba hid in the shadow of one of the darkest flyovers in the city counting the currency of his conspiracy, the past soon forgotten like a man's first breath after birth.

If modern medicine could help the aged man survive death by amputation, it had nothing in it to spare him of internal pains. For days, weeks and months long and self-wasting he lay, the unfitted arms of his replica lying by his side, tears streaming down his cheeks — no hands to wipe them for him.

Five kilometres away from Mvan, in the 30th floor of a fifty-storey building, in the Governor's office stood a life-like statue. Its hair was unkempt, its nose broad, its eyes tiny and its lower lip thick. It unfortunately had no arms. Anybody who happened to find themselves in that office was immediately attracted by this statue's exquisite beauty. 'By the living God whose creation is it?' People inevitably asked the Governor. This always filled the Governor with a kind of feeling which neither finds its place in resentment nor in remorse. The people's remarks not only reminded him of the old man whom he had killed, but more so of the course for which he had laid down his life.

How he wished he could discard the statue and forget everything it resurrected. But how could he? Whether or not he feared or felt uncomfortable with the realities trailed by this statue, his secret admiration for its beauty impelled him to share his office with it.

…Yaoundé, 2153 A.D.

THE VISIT
Oscar Chenyi Labang

It was about evening. The sun was drowning in the mind of the Ngoketunjia hill. Fresh breeze streamed downwards from the slopes of the Sabga hill. A worried dark cloud hung oppressively above the village. This however, was not noticeable to those in Tih Kungwe's compound partly because they were very concerned with preparations for the visit and also because smoke teaming out of the kitchen windows had formed a first sky. Women, sweating in different degrees, went in and out of the houses like soldier ants on a transfer trip. And young men gathered with rapidity like debris at the source of a great river. Yes, Tih Kungwe's compound was the source of the river for that day. It was weingang, the village market day, and all feet from the market squares marched towards his compound. All the wounded paths in Mbaghang meandered to the one leading to that compound. The compound had one main building at the entrance, and a vast yard with broken clay pots, half woven mats, and broken statues under a nkeng plant at the centre. Three smaller buildings, each with a kitchen adjacent to it, stood facing the main one. These buildings belonged to Tih Kungwe's three wives. It was from the kitchens that the smoke which had blinded the eye of the sky came out. This was a sign that all the women in the compound were in a harmonious and jubilant frame of mind. To them, at long last the visit was going to hold. They were going to have another companion in the compound.

Weingang, the market day, is usually the day for such visits because people hardly go to the farm. If it weren't on this day, it was on weinkoh, the country-Sunday. This weingang was the day on which they had planned to effect the visit. Time and time again attempts had been made to embark on the visit, but had always failed. The reasons had always been flimsy and as such had created in Kungwe a feeling that every other day attempt will end in a failure. The idea of the visit had become to him a boring subject and he hardly paid attention to anyone who wanted to say anything about it. His mind had worked and his feelings had been strained to the extent that this day meant nothing to him. Whether it was going to work today or not was of little concern to him. Even attempts by his friends and peers could not raise enough vim and vigour in the nerves of his dying mind. It was the day for them to give him the support and prove to him that as peers, they love him and want him to be a successful man.

It was the tradition in the village for young men to pull their strength together and participate in whatever project one of them had. They were used to assisting friends during the farming or the harvesting season and even in building houses. It was time for one to know whether he has people behind him or not. On such occasions, all the young men in the quarter assembled in the village square nearest to the compound of the young man or of his parents or at an agreed upon spot. It was usually before the eldest cock comes out to announce the breaking of day. From there, they will race to the farm. Some whistling. Some chanting. Some telling tales. Everyone was in a heroic mood, filled with determination and ready to work at any length. They had shared such moments together especially with Kungwe. He was known for animating other friends' occasions. His turn had come and so everybody was ready to put in his best. They were aware that this visit had been postponed more than twice but they did not think that it was enough reason for Kungwe to be sad. They therefore did all they could to put him in an acceptable mode for such a visit.

Kungwe and his friends sat in the central room of the main building in the company of some elders. In the room there was a bamboo chair designed to provide relaxation for an old man. No person, whether from that household or a visitor, ever sat on it. This was Tih Kungwe's chair and it was said that it was on that chair that he had hid his *nfang*. Besides it, though not too close was another chair of similar design. In it was Pa Ngeh, an old man. He had a heavy beard and a rough moustache like that of a he goat. Time had formed the muscles of his forehead into ridges. The white hair he wore over the face was proof that the wisdom of time never passed him by. As a Tih-Torh, a noble who assist the quarter head to rule the quarter, he had proven his sense of nobility, wisdom and social justice. The discussion of the young men fell on his ageing mind like drops of rain on the hot breast of the desert. He listened to the boys with keen interest, nursed his wisdom, summoned his wits, coughed, and leaned forward. Then, in his usual poetic and witty mood, Pa Ngeh began: 'Some wise men of our time have most aptly described love to be nothing but an irrational desire caused by a passion which enters the heart through wanton thoughts'. He coughed in jerky halves, removed a small cup of snoff from the left pocket of his jumpa and then scooped some of the stuff with the nail of his right thumb. He blocked one nostril with the left thumb, and sniffed the stuff into his brain. Then, closed his reddening eyes for a few seconds and sneezed with the forced of a mad horse. Opening his eyes, he continued 'Now, my age passes me by like a deer crosses its shadow. Time is wisdom, yet time is what we lack. So the wisdom of the ages I must dispense to your time before time catches up with me. Since we are about to embark on the visit to my old friend, Pa Ndenge, I will tell you one of the many stories that has kept the wisdom of our ancestry alive, and that has guided our homes since Ilungfung Kangbeche combined will power and inspiration with the magical strength of Felanteu to settle our people here…. When a calabash of oil breaks in the banda and drips directly into the cooking pot, then the Gods of that home are at peace….'

So saying, he leaned back with great effort, with groans of age, and began thus:

'Such are the stories that a father tells his sons when he notices that the nerve at their groans has started emitting heat. It is the role of the farmer to peg his yam tendril to avoid being trapped in between someday. A young man, when he takes for himself a wife, must act in precisely the same fashion that is never to let her get the upper hand, lest, when some time afterward he may desire to keep her in his order, he may find such a task beyond his powers and be forced to follow in her way for the rest of his life. I propose therefore to relate to you the story of two brothers to bring truth to this idea only if you would (out of your wanton youthfulness) grant me a kind and gracious hearing. I remember the late Chief very often said, 'A man who fails to lick his lips should not blame the hamattan for drying them…'.

A great time ago, about when the great warrior Felanteu kissed the earth of our forefathers, there lived in this village of Nsei two brothers who were both given to the trade of craft but who by lineage loved some husbandry. It was known among the villagers that their mother, when she was a maiden, hid behind a tree at night and washed a bad juju passing by. This act rendered her barren, but her beauty and dancing skill during a festival gladdened the heart and found favour in the eyes of the son of the god of fertility, Fungbekoh, who savoured her nakedness and in return watered her stony womb.... The boys grew to men of stature and skill. Great was their craft. People from all over the plains of Ngoketunjia and beyond came to glory the beauty and buy. The royalty developed great love for their handiwork and so gave them the honour to weave from the tips of their fine fingers royal mats and mould from the skin of their smooth palms royal vessels. Of these sons of Pa Nkoh one was called Beye and the other Kebra. There was great resemblance, love and friendship among them that anyone seeing them in the first instance would take them for twins.

Beye, who was the younger in years and fairer in disposition, took as wife a certain Nyingmeh, the daughter of a hunter. She was a very fair and lovely maiden, but somewhat over-flighty in honour. After the wedding was over and the bride brought home, Beye found himself completely dominated by the power of her beauty that it seemed to him that she must be beyond comparison. Forthwith, he fulfilled any demand that she made upon him. As the market days went by, Nyingmeh grew so arrogantly haughty and masterful that she took little or no reckon of her husband. If he should ask his wife to do one thing, she would, without delay, do something else, and whenever he told her to come here, she went there, and laughed at everything he said. Because the foolish fellow saw only through his own foolish eyes, he could neither pluck up enough courage to reproach her nor seek a remedy for his mistake. He let her go her way and work her will in everything according to her pleasure. Many seasons passed and Beye continued to live in the foolish realm he had created for himself.

Before another season of rain passed away, Kebra took as wife the other daughter of the hunter by the name of Bongwe; a damsel no less comely of person than her sister, Nyingmeh. When the wedding feast was over and the wife taken home to her husband's house, Kebra brought forth a pair of men's trousers and two battle sticks. Placing them on the ground before her, he said: 'Bongwe, my dear wife, this is a pair of trousers and two battle sticks, take one of the sticks and I will take one. We will fight over this pair of trousers to see who shall wear it. The one who wins in the fight shall be the wearer of the trousers and the one who loses shall henceforth yield obedience to the winner'. 'Ah, my lovely husband' Bongwe answered in a gentle voice 'What do you mean by such words? Are not you the husband, and I the wife? Ought not a wife bear herself obediently towards her husband? How could I ever bring myself to do such a foolish thing as this, to wrestle with my husband over trousers? Wear the trousers; surely they will fit on you better than they will on me'. 'I, then,' said Kebra 'will wear the trousers and be the husband, and you as my dearly beloved wife, will always hold yourself in obedience to me. But take care that you keep the same mind and do not hanker after taking the husband's role and giving me that of the wife. Such licence you will never get from me'. In her prudent manner, Bongwe confirmed all that she had said and Kebra, on his part, handed over to her the entire governance of the house, and committed all his wealth to her keeping, making known to her the order he desired to have in his household…"

There is ululation and singing outside, as the women welcome one of the elderly females of the family. They had finished cooking the food needed for the visit, and some who do not know how to idle for long had engaged in the female trade of gossip. All that they were waiting for now was the arrival of Pa Kungwe. He had travelled to Mbeka to buy *meloh fuuh*; for it was known all over the plain that good palm wine for such occasion could only come from Mbeka. It was even said among the elders that ancestral spirits respond faster to white stuff that comes from this village. The singing and ululation of the women distracted the company of youth and elders who were buried in the story of Pa Ngeh. Kungwe sat buried in thought. The distraction from the women outside meant little to him. His mind was a battery on charge, thoughts criss-crossing madly. However, the others quickly gained back their focus and turned to Pa Ngeh with more eager ears.

"… A little time after this, Kebra said to his wife 'Bongwe, come with me. Let me show you my animal farm and the way you should handle them should you at any time have to put your hand to such work'. There at the farm he asked his wife "what do you think about these my goats and sheep? They are handsome and finely tended? Bongwe affirmed that they were. Picking up a whip Kebra said 'now see how docile and handy they are'. Then he began to touch each indicating to what direction they were to move and they moved obediently. Now there was among the goats one fungoh with a shapely chin and a beautiful face but vicious and lazy at the same time. Kebra went up to this goat and gave it a sharp cut with the whip and cried out 'go over there' but the animal took no heed of the whip and refused to do anything his master ordered. Realising the beast's stubbornness, Kebra fell on it with a stick and hit with such strength that he soon ran out of energy. The fungoh proved more stubborn now than ever, and so in a violent rage Kebra drew a cutlass out of his shield and instantly slew the animal.

What Kebra had done, moved Bongwe with pity for the animal and she cried out 'Ah my husband! You have killed a goat so shapely to look at? Surely it was a great pity to have slain him in this way'. Strongly moved by passion, Kebra made a reply: 'Know then that all those who eat my *kebang* and refuse to do my will must hope to be paid in exactly the same coin as the goat'. Bongwe, when she heard these words, was greatly distressed and in her mind... '...what a wretched and miserable woman I am! What an evil day it was for me when I met this man! I believed I had chosen a man of good sense for my husband. I have become the prey of this brutal fellow. Behold how for little or no fault he killed this beautiful *fungoh*!' Thus she went on, grieving sorely to herself for she knew not why her husband had spoken in this wise.

As a result of what had passed, Bongwe fell into such fear and terror of her husband that she would tremble all over at the very sound of his footstep. Whenever he demanded any service of her, she would carry out his wishes straightway. Indeed she would understand his meaning even before he might open his mouth, and never a cross word passed between them.

Beye, who, on account of the great love he had for his brother Kebra, often visited the house of the latter, and dined and supped there. He observed the manners and carriage of Bongwe and being astonished thereat... 'Great God! Why was it not my lot to have Bongwe for my wife as is the good luck of my brother Kebra? See how nimbly she manages the house, and goes about her business without any uproar! See how obedient she is to her husband, and how she carries out every wish of his! But my wife, miserable fellow that I am, does everything in as vile a fashion as possible'.

On one occasion, by the working of chance, Beye and Kebra were in company. Out of distress, Beye spoke to his brother: 'Kebra, my brother, you are aware of the love that there is between us. Now, on this account, I would gladly learn what is the method you have followed in the training of your wife. She is altogether obedient to you, and treats you in such a loving wise. Now I, however gently I may ask Nyingmeh to do anything, I find that she always stubbornly refuses to answer me, and, beyond this does the exact opposite to what I asked her to do'. Smiling, Kebra told him word after word the way he used when first he brought his wife home. He counselled Beye to go and do the same and to see whether he might also succeed, adding that, in case this remedy should not be efficient, he would not know what other course to recommend.

Beye was well pleased with the advice and having taken his leave, he went away. Once he reached his house, he called his wife and brought out a pair of his trousers and two sticks following exactly as Kebra had recommended. When Nyingmeh saw what he was doing she laughed and called it a ridiculous fancy, noting to Beye that his trick was beside the purpose because it is evident that a man and not a woman should wear trousers. Beye made no answer but went ahead to lay down the rule for the regulation of his household. Nyingmeh was astonished by the humour of her husband and so mocked him even more and more. Still her husband kept silence. Taking her to his animal farm, he did with a fine goat everything which Kebra had done and in the end he slew it. When Nyingmeh saw what her husband had done, she was convinced in her own mind that he had lost his wits. She spoke unto her husband: 'By your faith, tell me husband, what crazy humours are these that have risen in your head? What is the true meaning of all this foolishness you are doing without thinking of the issue? Perhaps, it is your ill fate to have gone mad'. Then, Beye answered: 'I am not mad. I have made up my mind that anyone who lives at my charges and will not obey me shall be treated in such fashion as you have seen me use this morning towards my goat'. 'Ah, wretched fool!' Nyingmeh burst out 'It must be clear to you that your goat was nothing but a poor beast to allow itself to be killed in this manner. What is the full meaning of this whim of yours? Perhaps you think you can deal with me as you have dealt with the goat? If such is your belief then you are greatly mistaken. You put your hand much too late to the task of setting things in order after the fashion you desire. The bone is hard. The sore is now ulcerated and there is no cure at hand. You should have been more prompt in compassing the right of these curious wrongs of yours. What profit do you think you will get from them? None, as long as I am a living woman'.

Listening to his wife, Beye knew in his heart that his effort had miserably failed. So, he made up his mind, greatly to his chagrin, to put up patiently with his wretched lot till death should come to release him. Nyingmeh, when she discovered how little her husband's plan had turned to his advantage, resolved that if in the past she had worked her own will with the finger she will henceforth work it with the arm...."

Pa Ngeh ceased, and leaned back in his chair with satisfaction. He had driven the message into the young men and could read its effects on their faces and postures. A moment of silence passed and not a soul moved. One could hear the heavy breathing of the young men as their hearts pounded against their rib. Beside this, only the sharp cry of the owl from the trees in the ancestral grove could be heard.

'You are right Pa Ngeh', Pa Njah, who had followed the story from besides the doorpost with deepening keenness, broke the silence. 'Not even the fierceness of approaching flames can force a chameleon to change its steps. A woman headstrong by nature would rather die a thousand times than change the path which she has deliberately marked out for herself'. The company of youth that crowded the room breathed a breath of relief almost at once, as though they had lived the hell of Beye with him. A sign of strain flashed through Kungwe's face as he struggled to come to terms with the experience. He remembered that he once heard his father say that a man who does not have authority in his house was simply a slave to his wife.

'Here comes my good friend, the brave son of the son of the great warrior' announced Pa Njah standing up. The young men jumped up and out at once. They were used to this genealogical reference to Tih Kungwe. They received the kegs of palm wine and took them to an inner room. The women instantaneously got busy with arranging the different items. Tih Kungwe, after greeting his friends, entered the room into which the young men had entered with the wine. He removed a traditional cup from an age beaten raffia bag hanging behind the door, blew its inside twice and poured some wine into it. Standing a few steps from the doorpost that leads to the back yard, and looking straight into the dark forest that stretched in front of him he muttered a few words, poured the wine three times on the ground; uttered some more words and poured the wine three times again. He then smiled and entered the house to join his friends.

As food was being served to Tih Kungwe, he announced with some air of pride that the visit was set for eight o'clock, and so they had only slightly above half an hour left to be there. He was proud that at last his son Kungwe was going to join the club of responsible men. He was going to be a man, giving commands and receiving positive reactions. It was a great day for him that he was leading his kindred for a visit to Pa Ndenge; a visit that was to end with one more head coming under his roof. When Kungwe saw the pride and vim in his father, it occurred to him that truly it was his day. A new verve of joy flew into his nerves and everyone around could see that love had taken control of Kungwe. He whistled some love sounds that were common among his peers and smiled elaborately at whoever came around. Even enemies could have received a generous smile from Kungwe at that moment. In a great hurry, he and his friends got everything set, and his father announced the departure for the visit.

Sour Juice

Sammy Oke Akombi

The trees had grown into maturity. The fruits were beginning to ripen, large and juicy as they clustered in the branches. Some tall, some quite tall and others not quite. Each time Jacobo looked at them a current of hope and happiness ran from his brain through his heart down to his limbs. Like the legendary lizard, he would nod several times, hit his chest and say to himself: 'I've done it, I've done it, to be the owner of all these luscious fruits. Whoever gave me the initiative, resourcefulness and foresight must be divine. I think I have every right to boast success. I've done it.'

Jacobo had hardly achieved anything in his career as a public servant and that had been a great source of frustration for him. Ever since he got employed as an administrative staff in the Ministry of the Interior, he had never been given any assignment that could make him express himself like an intellectual and feel satisfied. He always thought that his education had been a huge waste of time, for it had been hugely put into disuse. His consolation had been a five hectare orange farm, which had given him something to live for and also look up to. He spent a lot more of his time on it and even went as far as sometimes having a conversation with the trees. So, when the fruits were bubbling in the trees like well formed breasts on the chest of a sweet sixteen, Jacobo couldn't wait to have the first harvest done.

It was a Saturday, so Jacobo mobilized his entire family and everyone went to the farm for the first harvest. The ripe fruits were carefully plucked off the clusters and neatly put in bags. There were ten bags altogether, each containing about sixty oranges. Before carting the bags away, the family decided to sit in the farm house – a thatched roof hut — and be the first to taste the fruits of their labour. Jaocobo's wife, Rosana selected seven juicy oranges and peeled them carefully. When she had finished, she handed an orange to each member of the family neatly cutting an opening. Almost simultaneously, everyone squeezed the content of their fruit into their mouth and strangely enough they spat out the juice immediately. Jacobo, who had equally spat the juice out could not help asking what the matter was?

'The oranges taste sour,' said Rosana.

'Yes they do,' chorused the rest of the family.

Jacobo was dumbfounded. He wondered why all seven juicy looking oranges should produce sour juice. He ordered his wife to randomly select seven other fruits and peel. She did and the experience was exactly the same. He still had the courage to make the family go through a third trial and it was nothing different.

At this point Jacobo felt his hopes flying off his chest. Unconsciously, he put his left thumb in his mouth and shortly after he started biting the nail, even chewing it.

'No!' he exclaimed, 'this can't be true. It can't be true!'

He ordered for a fourth trial but it failed to bring back the hope that he needed so badly. The family plodded their way back home far worse off than they had been before they came for the harvest.

Back home, Jacobo had become restless. There was nothing around him that pleased him. Not even Rosana, his wife. He decided he would contact the Divisional chief of Agricultural services. Unfortunately, it was a weekend and the man had gone to his village. He had to wait for Monday. At exactly eight o'clock that Monday, Jacobo left for the Agricultural Officer's. He found him in his office and they both examined all the possibilities that might have caused the sour taste of the fruits. They arrived at nothing, worth tackling.

'Was it the land?' Jacobo thought aloud as he stepped out of the office. It had been family land and it had been given to him with the blessing of every member of the family. The soil was good and the trees had grown healthily. As for the fertilizers which had been used on the farm, nothing proved that the substance could affect plants in such a negative way.

The situation was so worrying to Jacobo that he decided to go to his village, which was a couple of kilometres from the town, to complain to the oldest man who invariably was the wisest. The man had been his father's best friend when he was alive.

'Good afternoon, old one,' Jacobo began.

'Good afternoon, my son. What's it you want from me. You hardly ever come here on a week day, like this.'

'I've come to you because something very strange has happened to me and I believe it's your wisdom that will put my spirits back on course.'

'Sit down first of all my son. Do you need some cool water?'

'Yes, that's very thoughtful.'

Jacobo drank two cups of water, took a deep breath and felt much relaxed.

'Now, can you tell me what this strange thing that has happened to you is?'

'Yes, of course, old and wise one. I've spent all that I have in terms of money, material and time on a farm back in town and the fruits that I get from it are sour, very sour. Every single fruit is sour. That's rather strange.'

'It's surely very strange. All the fruits sour?' asked the old man.

'Yes old one, all the fruits sour.' Jacobo affirmed.

'Have you found out about the soil and other factors?'

'Yes, old one.'

'Did you give food to your ancestors before you started the farm?'

'Yes, I did.'

'Before you planted the seedlings, were they blessed?'

'Yes, they were.'

'Now, What about the money to carry out the project? How did you get it?'

'How I got the money? That was a long time ago.'

'Yes, it was a long time ago but you should still remember how you got it. What was the source of the money.'

'Source of money?'

'Yes, source of money. How did it come about? Was it a bank loan?'

'No, not at all. It wasn't a loan. It was some sort of manna. Yes, manna from heaven.'

'Manna from heaven! That must be very interesting. Tell me more about this manna eh…eh money from heaven,' the old man said, looking very interested.

'Well,' said Jacobo 'it sometimes happens, you know. For example there was this couple, somewhere in one of the countries of the white man, who got up one morning and found their courtyard green with banknotes. Husband and wife spent the whole morning putting the notes together in bags. When they had finished they sat together to consider the next line of action. First, they established that they were genuine notes and then invited the police and the press to tell them their story. It was concluded that a suitcase of money might have fallen off a flying aircraft, bursting open and spilling out its content in the courtyard. Adverts were therefore put in different newspapers, requesting anyone who might have lost money to come up and claim it, but nobody did. After one, two and even three months, the police officially declared the couple the sole proprietors of the money. Wouldn't you call that manna from heaven?' asked Jacobo.

'Indeed it was manna from heaven and your story has just reminded me of another story I know very well. In those days, when my son was working in the capital city and I was staying with him, following up my pension file, he returned home one day looking very worried. When I asked him what the matter was, he said that something strange had happened to his boss. There had been a fault in the electrical installation in his official residence and he had given instructions that it should be verified and repaired. So an electrician was invited to do the job. He had to go into the ceiling where he did not only identify the electrical fault but also discovered something unusual. Five-figure banknotes had been neatly packed in cartons at one corner of the ceiling. He carefully climbed down, went to a nearby store and bought a large *Ghana-must-go* bag and climbed back into the ceiling with it and filled it neatly. He corrected the electrical fault and slipped out of the house without any one taking much notice of him. When the boss returned in the evening, he was only too happy that the fault had been corrected. It was only on the seventh day that he discovered what had befallen him.'

On that Sunday morning, while his wife and children had gone to church to worship their God, he had remained at home to worship his — money. As soon as he was all by himself, he got a ladder and climbed into the ceiling. When he set his eyes on the spot where he had kept his God, he knew something had gone wrong. He hit the torch, he had brought with him, several times hoping it would light the place better but the situation did not change. He went on his knees, spread out his arms feeling every corner but he felt no banknote. He sniffed and sniffed every corner but he smelt nothing like a banknote. His breathing had almost stopped when something told him to be a man. Gently, he found his way out of the ceiling. He went to his private living room and slumped in a couch brooding over his money.

'My money, ah my money,' he thought. 'hundreds of millions in maximum notes, all gone. Seems like a dream. A very bad dream.'

He did not have time enough to weep over his lost wealth because his wife and children had just returned from church. They found him in an unusual way.

'What's wrong with you honey?' asked his wife.

'It's the gastric pain. It has started again.'

'Not again!' She exclaimed. 'Should I call Dr Wakawa?'

'No, don't bother. I hope the pains will go, even if not as swiftly as they had come. What I need now is to be alone and have some sleep.'

He got out of the couch and sluggishly walked to his bedroom. He lay down for a long, long time.

'Well,' said Jacobo, 'that was the electrician's own manna from heaven'

'Do you think? It could have been manna from hell. The source of the money was unknown,' said the old one.

'What do you mean unknown? Was it not from the ceiling of your son's boss?'

'Yes, it was. But tell me, is the inside of a ceiling, the place for hundreds of millions of banknotes?'

'I see your point, old one.'

'I'm glad you understand. One has to be careful about such money because genuine happiness can be achieved only when one earns what they have. Remember you still haven't told me about your own manna from heaven.'

'You know, old one,' Jacobo began, 'my late father loved me so much and he believed a lot in educating his children. He had always told us that earthly salvation was in education. So he sacrificed a lot to send me to Australia for further education. After my postgraduate degree in Economics, I decided to return home and be useful to my country. But then, things did not work out as I had thought. After my return, I sojourned in the unemployment train for two years. I was almost getting mentally disturbed when a providential act of the President got me out of the train. I then stumbled on the trail of a career in the Ministry of the Interior.

'While in the capital city, compiling the necessary documents for posting, I ran into a friend who was carrying out the same exercise. He had returned from the Soviet Union a year earlier. As soon as we had finished exchanging greetings, he said:

'Tell you what? It's raining money somewhere in the city.'

'How's that?' I asked

'I've just pocketed a whooping one million five hundred thousand francs and it is like this. I was going to deposit my recruitment documents when someone cornered me and asked if I had studied abroad and I said yes. He then asked me to prove it. I became suspicious and asked what he was up to. He took me aside and said that there was this lady who was the owner of a transit company and she had won the contract to transport the luggage of all those who were abroad and had been recruited through the providential act of the President. I told him I did not qualify because I had already returned home and I had been recruited while already in the country. He said it did not matter where I had been recruited. What mattered was simply proof that I had studied abroad. A simple attestation from the University where I had studied was enough. I looked at him and asked if he was sure. He assured me and I simply gave him a photocopy of my result attestation from Patrice Lumumba Friendship University, Moscow and then I indicated my name on the recruitment list. He gave me an address and asked me to meet him the following day. When I got there that day, behold I was given some documents to sign and ten minutes later I was smiling home with the sum I had told you about in my pocket.'

'So old one,' said Jacobo, 'when my friend told me that story, it sounded almost like a fairy tale but he took out ten thousand francs from his pocket and gave me to help myself. He also gave me the name and address of the man who had informed him about the transaction. The following day, I rushed there and submitted my certificate from Melbourne and indicated my name on the recruitment list. My appointment was much longer. I was asked to come after two weeks. I wondered why it had to be two weeks in my own case. But it gave me time to consider the rationale behind the whole transaction. In my own case I had been through with Melbourne, two years before, and since then I had been looking for a job. Then the providential act came and my name figured on the list, and there was someone going to claim that she had transported my luggage from Australia. She was going to be paid I didn't-know-how-much but the hope was that I was going to get something out of it. No doubt, my friend had said it was raining money. The two weeks came by and I went to the transit company, signed some papers and I was given the same sum of money as my friend from Moscow. I thought I was going to have more considering the distance between the country and Melbourne. However, in things like that logic was absent. I pocketed the money and went home. The idea that I did not actually deserve the money worried me for some time but I soon went over it especially because there had been many other beneficiaries like me. There was even the case of someone who had had a job earlier in the administration in a different capacity and had been earning a salary. Then his name came up in the list of beneficiaries of the providential act. He had studied in a neighbouring country and had returned home three years earlier. He too qualified for the luggage transit transaction and he pocketed his own share. In this regard, I felt a bit more at ease with the money and then dubbed it manna from heaven. Before I got posted, I took the money home and told my father about it and that I wanted to invest it in agriculture. That's how he got the family to give me the land on which the farm is. So old one, that's it. The manner in which I got my manna from heaven.'

The old and wise one shook his head and asked, 'My son, do you know if that transit company is still existing?'

'No idea. I haven't had anything to do with it ever since I got the money.'

'I would be surprised if it still exists. Companies that thrive on corruption don't thrive for long. What I can say is that the company had arranged a dirty deal with some top officials, taking advantage of the fact that some of the people who had been recruited through the providential act were still abroad, and they had to be encouraged to return home. So, that manna of yours was dirty money, which you did not deserve. My son, dirty money may profit in the short term but never in the long term.'

'But old one what would I have done? It was raining money as my friend had said. Would it not have been foolish of me not to have taken advantage of the rain?'

'My son, it is not because everyone is taking advantage of something that you too must take advantage of it. You told the story of a couple who got up and found their courtyard full of money. Did they take advantage of the situation? You yourself said it, they duly informed the police and the press. So my son, there's no doubt that the oranges from your farm have produced sour juice because they were cultivated on sour money. Never trust money that you haven't sweated for.'

Notes on the Contributors

Sammy Oke Akombi is Cameroonian, born in Tinto, Manyu division, Southwest Province. He went to the teacher's college in Batibo. At the end of the course he realized he could share ideas through writing. He did his A-Levels at the Bilingual Grammar School, Buea. In 1981 he enrolled at the Faculty of Education, University of Lagos, Nigeria. He graduated in 1984 with a B.A. (Honours) in Education, and started a career in teaching. In 1989 he went to the University of Warwick (U.K.), whence he graduated in 1990 with an M.A. in English Language Teaching. In October of that year, he started work with the Bilingual Training Programme, and today he is the Director of the Southwest Provincial Linguistic Centre, Buea. His published literary works include *Grandma's Daughter, The Raped Amulet, The Woman Who Ate Python* and *Beware the Drives*. He is an honorary fellow in writing of the University of Iowa, U.S.A.

Wirndzerem G. Barfee was born on 1 August 1975 in Kumbo, Bui Division, North West Province of Cameroon. He attended GHS Kumbo and CCAST Bambili during his secondary and high school days. He read Mass Communication at the University of Jos, Nigeria, holds a B.A. in Linguistics and an M.A. in American Literature from the University of Yaoundé I where he is currently doing his pre-doctoral D.E.A. with critical interests in eco-criticism and feminism. A two-time participant in the British Council/ Lancaster University CROSSING BORDERS pan-African creative writing programme (2004/2006), he was earlier selected to participate in the BBC/BRITISH COUNCIL Environmental Writing Workshop in 1996. Recently, with a national grant, he published a poetry collection, *Bird of the Oracular Verb* (Iroko Publishers, 2008). He has a passion for songwriting and has written songs in Lamnso (his native tongue), English and French, for two local artists. A graduate of the National School of Administration and Magistracy, specialising in public finance, he works with the Ministry of Finance.

Oscar Chenyi Labang is one of Cameroon's budding talents: poet, critic, short story writer and playwright. He holds an M.A. in Modern British Poetry and a D.E.A. in Modern Anglo-American Poetry and currently working on a Ph.D thesis on the intersections of literature and philosophy with particular focus on the philosophical concept of nihilism and modernist Anglo-American Poetry. He is former President of the Yaoundé University Poetry Club and winner of the Bernard Folon Poetry Competition (2005). His publications include contributions to *Imagination of Poets: Anthology of African Poems* (2005) and *This is Bonamoussadi* (A Long Poem) (2008). He is editor of *Emerging Voices: Anthology of Young Anglophone Cameroon Poets*, and author of one critical work, *Riot in the Mind: A Study of John Nkemngong Nkengasong* (2008).

Ba'bila Mutia holds an M.A. in Creative Writing from the University of Windsor, Ontario, Canada, and a Ph.D in English from Dalhousie University, Nova Scotia, Canada. He teaches oral and written literatures, creative writing, advanced writing, and research methodology at the University of Yaoundé I. His short stories and poetry have featured in anthologies and reviews worldwide, and his work has been broadcast on the BBC. In 1993 Mutia was a guest of the Berlin Academy of Arts for an international short story reading. He has been a visiting Fulbright scholar in Western Washington University, Bellingham, USA (1996/97); visiting professor of African Literature, Bayreuth University, Germany (2000/01); and visiting professor of African literature and creative writing in Dickinson College, Carlyle, US (2003/04). Mutia is the author of *Whose Land?* (Longman); *Before This Time, Yesterday* (Silex/Nouvelles du Sud); 'Rain' in *A Window on Africa*; and 'The Miracle' in *The Heinemann Book of Contemporary African Short Stories*. His most recent poetry collection, *Coils of Mortal Flesh*, was released by Langaa Publishers in January 2008.

Florence Ndiyah was born in Njinikom in the North West province of Cameroon on 10 October 1976. After completing primary education at Government Bilingual Primary School, Yaoundé, she moved on to St Bede's College, Ashing Kom, and later to the University of Buea, Cameroon, where she obtained a B.Sc. in Microbiology/Laboratory Technology. Her professional exploits started with a job as a laboratory technician and continued to writing, first for a magazine and then a newspaper. She got into fiction in 2005 when she was selected for the 2005/06 session of the British Council *Crossing Borders* creative writing project. With a diploma in copywriting, she presently works as freelance writer and communication officer to some local and international organisations. Her major product is a training manual for trainers which she co-authored for the International Labour Organisation, Cameroon, as a writer and trainer. She lives in Yaoundé.

Eunice Ngongkum was born in Kusu-Wum, in the Menchum Division of the North West Province of Cameroon. She attended Presbyterian School Wum, Government High School (now GBHS), Mbengwi, whence she proceeded to the then University of Yaoundé for undergraduate and postgraduate studies. In 2002, she obtained a Ph.D in African Literature and is currently Senior Lecturer in the Department of African Literature and Civilizations of the University of Yaoundé I. She has been a secondary school teacher of English Language and Literature for several years and is an active member of ACWA, the Association of Cameroon Anglophone Writers. Her first collection of short stories, *Manna of a Life Time and Other Stories*, was published by Editions Clé, Yaoundé, in 2007. A second; *Wen Men Nté*, has been accepted for publication in 2009. She is co-author of *Living English Power: A New Secondary English Course for Cameroon Schools*, and is equally a literary critic with a substantial number of articles in national and international journals. She is married and mother of five.

John Nkemngong Nkengasong is a playwright, fiction writer, poet and critic. Born in Lewoh Fondom in the Lebialem Division of the South West Province of Cameroon, he studied at Seat of Wisdom College, Fontem, and the University of Yaoundé I, where he obtained a Ph.D in English Poetry. Presently he is Associate Professor of Literature in the Department of English, University of Yaoundé I. He has been a Visiting Lecturer at the University of Dschang, part-time Lecturer at the *Ecole Normale Supérieure*, Yaoundé, Fulbright scholar at New York University, guest author at Corpus Christi College, University of Oxford, visiting academic at the University of Regensburg, Germany, and a participant at the International Writing Program at the University of Iowa, USA. He is the current president of the Anglophone Cameroon Writers' Association. His published works include *Black Caps and Red Feathers* (2001), *Across the Mongolo* (2004), *The Widow's Might* (2006), *W. B. Yeats and T. S. Eliot: Myths and the Poetics of Modernism* (2005), *A Stylistic Guide to Literary Appreciation* (2007), poems published in anthologies in Africa and the United States, and several scholarly articles in national and international journals.

Job Fongho Tende, a native of the North-West province of Cameroon, was born and bred in the Central province of the country. He is at present a Masters student in the English department of the University of Yaoundé I, studying commonwealth literature. Yaoundé and its mixture of people from all over the country, its several languages (French, English, pidgin, *franc-anglais* and some national languages), its socio-political atmosphere, have not left the budding writer uninfluenced. He has written over 150 poems, two drama pieces, a number of short stories and two short novels for teenagers, all of which are yet unpublished.

Mbuh Mbuh Tennu was born in 1966, and obtained his first degree in the then University of Yaoundé in 1987. By 1996, when he defended his *Doctorat de 3ème Cycle*, he was already a graduate assistant in the Department of English, where he was eventually recruited and has been teaching ever since. In 2003, he benefited from a Commonwealth scholarship award to do a Ph.D on D. H. Lawrence at the University of Nottingham (U.K.). Tennu has been writing since his undergraduate years, and was a Bernard Fonlon Society literary competition laureate in 1991 and 1992 consecutively, for the short story 'Not I Alone' and poem 'Oracle of Tears' respectively. He is also a founding member of the Anglophone Cameroon Writers Association (ACWA). An unpublished drama piece, *Who's Afraid of Mongo Wa Swolenka?*, was performed by the Yaoundé University Poetry Club to commemorate the first anniversary of the execution of the Nigerian activist Ken Saro Wiwa. Some of Tennu's poems have appeared in local and American newspapers. He has an unpublished historical novel, *The Death of Asobo Ntsi*, and is currently working on a semi-autobiographical novel, *In the Shadow of My Country*.

About the Editor

Emma Dawson currently lectures at Keele University. She works at the intersection of postcolonial writing, pedagogy and the emergent field of World Englishes literature. She has published a number of academic articles in the field, and her Ph.D addressed the teaching of World Englishes literature in schools in England. As a result of her studies she published *Read Around*, a ground-breaking series for secondary schools (CCC Press, 2008). She is the general Editor of CCCP's World Englishes Literature imprint, and in its fiction series is currently editing anthologies of short stories from Nigeria, Uganda and Kenya (forthcoming, 2009).

9 781905 510214